"I don't know about that, but at least the music."

"A good start," he said. "I'll be happy to fill in the blanks whenever you like."

"Good. I plan to hold you to that," she promised.

At the moment, he would have just settled for holding her. The thought of their bodies touching had a rippling effect through Anderson, causing his temperature to rise. Was she feeling the vibe, too?

After the meal, Anderson walked Holly to her car. He wanted more than anything to kiss her. Something told him she felt the same.

He leaned in slowly and grazed her lips.

Holly felt his lips on hers and was quick to reciprocate. She had been hoping Anderson would kiss her, as it seemed the perfect way to end what had been a pleasant date. The kiss, which lasted for several scintillating seconds, wasn't a disappointment in the slightest. She liked that he wasn't pushing for too much, too soon, and was respectful in giving them both something to look forward to the next time.

In her mind, it was a given that there would be a next time. But were they on the same wavelength?

Books by Devon Vaughn Archer

Harlequin Kimani Romance

Christmas Heat
Destined to Meet
Kissing the Man Next Door
Christmas Diamonds
Pleasure in Hawaii
Private Luau
Aloha Fantasy
Love is in the Air

DEVON VAUGHN ARCHER

is a bestselling author of many Harlequin Kimani Romance novels. These include *Love is in the Air* and three stories that take place on different Hawaiian islands, including *Pleasure in Hawaii, Private Luau* and *Aloha Fantasy*. He is also the author of the Kimani holiday classics *Christmas Diamonds* and *Christmas Wishes*. Archer was the first male author to write for Harlequin's Kimani Arabesque line with the moving love story *Love Once Again*. The author has also written a number of bestselling urban and mainstream fiction, including *Danger at Every Turn* and *The Hitman's Woman,* as well as hot-selling young adult fiction, *Her Teen Dream* and *His Teen Dream.* To keep up with his latest news and upcoming books, follow, friend or connect with Devon Vaughn Archer on Twitter, Facebook, YouTube, LinkedIn, MySpace, Goodreads, LibraryThing and www.devonvaughnarcher.com.

Love is in the Air

DEVON VAUGHN ARCHER

HARLEQUIN® KIMANI™ ROMANCE

To "Sleeping Beautiful,"
my other half and gorgeous wife who taught me
the meaning of true love and a lifetime commitment.

And to my mother, Marjah A. Flowers,
and sister, Jacquelyn V. White, the other ladies in my life
who have provided the inspiration and support
to make me the person I am today.

ISBN-13: 978-0-373-86295-5

LOVE IS IN THE AIR

Copyright © 2013 by R. Barri Flowers

Recycling programs for this product may not exist in your area.

Printed in U.S.A.

HARLEQUIN®
www.Harlequin.com

Dear Reader,

I am happy to present to you my latest Harlequin Kimani Romance, *Love is in the Air*. It is sure to keep you engaged throughout.

When a weekend anchor and a legal consultant wind up sitting together on a flight to Houston, it is but the beginning of their romantic journey that will perhaps never bring the pair back down to earth.

The idea for this story was conceived from a visit to the airport and imagining two strangers finding romance by chance and a mutual desire to fall in love. Is your mind open enough to find romance in the air, if you clicked with your seatmate?

This wonderful romance will make you believe anything is possible with love.

I invite you as well to read my three recent Hawaii-themed romances, *Aloha Fantasy, Private Luau* and *Pleasure in Hawaii*.

Kind regards,

Devon Vaughn Archer

I would like to thank my wife, H. Loraine,
for her tireless devotion to me and my writing.
I would never have found my current success without
her presence in my world.

I also express appreciation to the Harlequin Kimani
editors and staff I have worked with for their
professionalism and support through the years.

Chapter 1

Saying goodbye was always the worst part of a trip for Holly Kendall. She was tongue-tied as she stood there at the Portland International Airport with her brother, Stuart, who was two years older at thirty-three, and his cute-as-a-button seven-year-old twin daughters, Dottie and Carrie. What was supposed to be a mid-August weekend trip from Houston had stretched into three days, but still seemed like far too little time. It would just give her an excuse to come back for a visit sooner rather than later.

"Well, guess you'd better get out of here, or you'll have us all in tears," Stuart said, scratching his pate under his short, dark hair.

"I suppose." Holly had sworn she would keep it together at this point. But could she help it if they were the only family she had, aside from her father? Their mother had died suddenly five years ago. A year later, Stuart's wife had left him to raise their daughters all by himself. Who said life was ever fair?

Holly bent down and gave the girls a hug and big kiss. "You take care of your daddy, you hear?"

"We will," Carrie said tearfully.

"Promise," Dottie followed.

"Good girls." Holly stood up and reached to hug Stuart, who towered over her five-foot-nine-inch frame. "Maybe next time Dad will come with me."

"Yeah, right," Stuart scoffed. "I can count on one hand the times he's visited since we've lived here."

"He doesn't like to be too far away from home," Holly said. "At least not since Mom passed away. But hey, never say never."

"I won't. And that includes never saying you won't meet Mr. Right and start your own family someday," Stuart said.

"I'll believe it when I see it." It wasn't that she had no faith such a person existed. It was more a matter of him never quite materializing in her busy world. She hadn't exactly given up trying. But between her work as a weekend anchor, volunteer work and hanging out with her friends, she honestly wasn't sure there was any time left in her life right now for a man.

Holly waved goodbye before going through security and heading for her gate. She had a half hour or so before boarding, so she stopped in a store and purchased an *Oregonian* newspaper, bottled water and some mints.

When she neared the gate, Holly could see that it would be a full flight. So what else was new these days as airliners consolidated and looked for every cost-cutting measure?

She saw an empty seat in the waiting area right next to a good-looking man. He was bald, well dressed and seemed quite content to stare off into space with his deep gray-brown eyes. Of course that changed when he saw her approaching and he gave her his undivided attention. A moment of self-consciousness swept over Holly as he assessed her from head to toe. She was dressed casually with little makeup, and her shoulder-length wavy black hair was in a convenient ponytail.

What difference does it make if I'm not at my best? she thought. *It's not like I'm trying to impress him or anything.*

"Is this seat taken?" she asked calmly.

"It is now," he said, an amused grin playing on his lips. He moved a briefcase over that had been sitting on the floor in front of the chair, clearing the way.

"Thank you." The instant she sat down, Holly got a whiff of the man's strong cologne. It was Obsession, which happened to be Stuart's favorite. She preferred something a bit more mellow and on the spicy side. But then she realized it wasn't her that he was trying to impress. He probably had a lady waiting when he reached his final destination.

Holly put the folded newspaper on her lap as she tried to get comfortable in the chair. The man beside her reached to grab the paper.

"You mind if I take a look at the sports section?" he asked.

She shot him a cold stare. Snatching it away, she responded, "Actually, I do mind. Maybe you should ask before you assume."

He cocked a thick brow. "Maybe I should have, but for some reason I didn't think you were into sports."

"That's beside the point," she said stiffly. "I prefer to be asked for something that belongs to me." In fact, she loved sports and had grown up with a father and brother who couldn't get enough football and basketball. They had passed their love for the games on to her, and she had always hated when other men assumed that she knew nothing about sports.

He chuckled. "My apologies. Would it be all right if I took a look at the business section? Or is that off-limits, too?"

Holly had the feeling he was being condescending. Did she not look like someone interested in business? Or did he simply think he was entitled to someone's property when he was perfectly capable of buying his own newspaper?

She met his eyes. "Look, I bought the paper to read myself, without having to share or wait till someone finishes a section when I'm ready to read it. I suggest you go over there and buy your own newspaper. They had plenty left."

"Are you always so possessive of what's yours?" he asked coldly.

"Only when someone's persistent and won't leave it alone."

He took a breath. "I can't believe we're squabbling over a damned newspaper."

"So let's not," she countered, "and we'll get along fine."

He laughed. "Yeah, whatever."

Holly sensed that he was irked and wondered if she should find another place to sit. Trouble was, there were no other empty chairs near the gate. So she was stuck there. Next to someone who probably thought she was acting like a bitch.

Perhaps she had overreacted. After all, it wasn't as if she couldn't share the paper while holding on to the front and entertainment sections, which she most wanted to read.

She pulled out the sports section and put it on his lap. "Keep it," she said. "I can get any sports news I need from my iPad."

He grinned, picking up the paper. "Thanks."

"Forget it." She opened up her water and took a drink before lifting up the entertainment section, trying her best to ignore him, but finding it impossible for some reason. Perhaps it was because she could tell from her periphery that he was staring at her. Against her better judgment, she stared back. "Is there something else you want?"

"Actually, there is…" His eyes narrowed. "You look strangely familiar."

I was wondering how long it would take for that to

come up, she thought. She was used to people recognizing her from television and pretty much took it in stride. This time would be no different.

"I get that a lot," she told him.

"Really?"

"Yes, it seems to be a great pickup line."

He chuckled. "I suppose. Not this time, though. Seriously, could we have met somewhere before, or—"

Holly had a mind to satisfy his curiosity and get back to reading the paper, but she knew that would likely open the door to more questions that invaded her personal space. "I doubt that," she assured him. "I never forget a face." She certainly would not have forgotten his, for better or worse.

"Neither do I," he insisted, staring at her. "Especially one so striking."

"Oh please…" Holly was somewhat flattered, but she had a feeling that he was a player who used lines that probably worked on most women. Not her, though. Many men had found her attractive, even beautiful. But in most instances, they were more interested in what was below the waist than above. Was that his intention, as well?

"Maybe we could start this conversation over," he said coolly. "My name's Anderson."

Holly looked at him as she considered the name. It somehow suited him, and maybe even piqued her interest a tad. Did he live in Portland? Houston? Or neither?

"Holly," she said simply.

"Nice to meet you, Holly."

"You too." She responded as she would to anyone she was talking to at the airport. Even if Anderson was drop-dead handsome and seemingly interested in her. Or was he simply just passing the time waiting for their flight to board?

Anderson Gunn tried to read the sports section. But the truth was, he was captivated by the beautiful lady seated next to him. Even without being overly dressed up or wearing much makeup, it was obvious that she had the complete physical package: tall and slender, with just the right amount of curves and bends. He liked her butterscotch complexion and heart-shaped faced. Her lips were full and seemingly created to be kissed. He imagined if her hair were down, it would be silky smooth were he to run his fingers through it.

Though his attraction to her was undeniable, there was more about her that piqued Anderson's curiosity. There was no question that he had seen her before. But where? Maybe at a bar? On the street? At a social event? Then it hit him like a bolt of lightning.

"Wait—" He leaned forward, peering into eyes that were like black pearls and just as enchanting. "You're Holly Kendall! You do the evening news on KJTW."

Holly frowned. "You've got me. Except that I'm the weekend anchor in the morning on KOEN."

Damn. Blew that one, he thought. "My apologies. To tell you the truth, I get most of my news from CNN and Fox, along with my iPhone. But I do catch some local news and recognized your face—albeit the wrong time and wrong channel."

"Don't worry, I won't hold it against you," she said, even if it bruised her ego just a bit. "It happens."

He feigned a sigh of relief. "Glad to hear that."

"So I take it you live in Houston?"

"Yep, born and raised there. Spent some time living in Dallas, Sacramento and Memphis along the way."

"I see." She wondered if he was a military brat. Or did his family just move around a lot?

"I'm guessing you grew up in Houston, too, by the accent." He'd detected it right away. It was subtle but unmistakable nonetheless, just as he supposed his accent was.

Holly raised a thin brow. By most accounts she didn't have an accent, per se. Especially not on the air. Admittedly, she did let her guard down somewhat when being herself and conceded that maybe she did have a slight Southern drawl.

"Yes, I'm from Houston," she said, sipping her water. "And I've never lived anywhere else, though I've traveled to quite a few different places."

"It's a great city to hang one's hat," Anderson said.

"I agree."

"You didn't happen to attend the University of Houston, did you?" Anderson asked.

"Yes, in fact, I did. I received my bachelor's and master's degrees in communication there," Holly said proudly. She looked at him, guessing he was about two or three years older. "Did you?"

"Yeah, I did my time there as an undergrad before moving on to the University of Houston Law Center."

Her eyes grew wide, impressed. "So you're a lawyer?"

"Not a practicing one," he told her, not wanting to bore her with the details of his change from a high-powered corporate attorney to a less stressful and time-consuming occupation. "Actually I'm a legal consultant."

Either way, Holly imagined that he was making good money. She wondered who he was spending it on. As if that was any of her business.

"Is that why you're in Portland?" she asked.

He nodded. "I have a client here. How about you?" He hoped to hell she didn't say she was carrying on a long-distance love affair, though he couldn't imagine any guy wanting to be that far apart from such a smoking-hot woman.

"I have a brother and two nieces living here. I was just up for a short visit."

"Cool." Anderson found that he'd lost all interest in reading the paper. Especially when he'd rather read into Holly Kendall and learn as much as possible about who she was. Would she be okay with that? Or would he be pressing his luck by continuing the conversation?

Before he could say anything else, Anderson's phone rang. He took it out and saw that it was his Portland client, Dodson Paul, who ran a very successful law firm.

Anderson frowned at Holly. "I have to take this."

She batted her lashes. "Don't let me stop you."

Holly watched him shoot to his feet before answering the call. It gave her a moment to further assess him. He was tall at around six-four, and appeared very fit, as though he worked out regularly. She thought his pecan complexion suited him, and his square-jawed face with a prominent nose and wide mouth only added to his physical appeal.

He stepped farther away, turning his back, as though to block anyone from hearing the conversation. Not that she wanted to hear him saying sweet things to his wife or girlfriend. A tiny piece of Holly felt envious, since she had no one at home waiting for her. But she had put loneliness on the back burner in favor of the rich life she had otherwise.

When it was announced that first-class passengers could board, Holly stood. It had been nice to have the brief chat with Anderson, but she doubted either of them had any room in their lives for one another in Houston.

She stood up and looked his way. He was so absorbed in his conversation that he didn't even notice. She grabbed her bag, leaving the paper behind, and took her place in line.

When Anderson got off the phone, he noticed that the plane was boarding. He also saw that Holly was gone. Damn—he hadn't gotten a chance to say goodbye.

Anderson grabbed his briefcase and headed for the plane. He definitely envisioned Holly as girlfriend material. She was gorgeous, sexy in an understated way, educated and obviously successful as a television personality.

But he seriously doubted that with her qualities she was just sitting around waiting for a man to pop into her life. He couldn't get that lucky. Could he?

In any event, he realized it probably didn't make much difference now since that window of opportunity had passed. For all he knew, she was sitting beside some dude on the plane who was busy trying to win her over.

Anderson boarded the plane. The moment he entered the cabin, he spotted Holly sitting all by her lonesome in a window seat in first class. It wasn't till he checked his boarding pass that he realized, against all odds, that she was his seatmate.

And she was occupying his seat.

He grinned when she looked up at him. "Well, hello again," he said.

"Hi." Holly colored a little from the intensity of his stare. She peeked past him as if trying to point out that other people were in line behind him, waiting for him to proceed down the aisle.

"Looks like we'll have time after all to finish the conversation we started," he said with a glint of amusement in his eyes.

"Excuse me?" Her lashes fluttered at the notion.

"We're sitting side by side," Anderson said. "Actually, if you check your boarding pass, you'll find that I have the window seat."

"Really?" Holly pulled the slip of paper out of her purse, clearly surprised that she was in the wrong seat. "My mistake. I'll be happy to move."

Anderson dismissed it with a wave of his hand. "Don't worry about it. I'm cool with the aisle seat."

"Are you sure?"

"Positive. It's easier for my long legs to get up and flex." He also liked the idea of her being effectively stuck on the inside so there was no escaping him. After tossing his bag in the overhead bin, he slid into the seat next to her. Suddenly the normally dull flight to Houston had gotten a lot more intriguing.

Chapter 2

The flight was a bit bumpy, which made Holly a little nervous. Not to say that she was a fearful flier, but they were 30,000 feet in the air and she didn't take anything for granted.

Somehow she felt comforted by Anderson's masculine presence, as though it was his job to make sure nothing bad happened to her. It was a silly thought, especially considering that his close proximity also made her a little nervous. She usually felt that way whenever she was attracted to a man. Since it had been a while since she could say that, she hadn't decided yet if that was a good or bad thing.

"Weekend morning anchor, huh?" Anderson commented, nursing a scotch on the rocks as he watched Holly sip some red wine.

"That's me." She wondered if he viewed that as a lesser position than anchoring the weekday noon news, which her good friend, Blythe Cramer, co-anchored with veteran newscaster Allan Kennedy.

"I have to be honest in saying that you're even more beautiful in person—and that's not a line."

"Thank you," Holly said, though still not sure if he was getting carried away with her looks. "But I'm not on television as an actress. I'm a serious journalist."

"And you do your job very well," he said, although he didn't get to see her often enough on his big-screen television. That would have to change. "There is one thing I've always been curious about when watching newscasters—"

"Hmm…do I really want to know?" she asked, half joking.

"When you're reporting all that bad news with murders, car accidents, robberies and the like, do you take that home with you or leave it at the job?"

Holly stared at him for a beat before offering a response. "Both," she said diplomatically. "Of course, you wouldn't be human if you could talk about such things and simply shut it off once you leave the desk. But, on the other hand, if you let it all get to you too much it would probably drive you crazy. Meaning you shouldn't be in broadcast journalism."

"Well-thought-out answer," Anderson said, impressed.

"Just telling you how I feel." She looked at him. "Do you take your work home, figuratively speaking?"

"I used to much more than I do now," he responded thoughtfully. "These days I try to keep my business and personal life as separate as possible, which isn't always easy."

"So what happened to make you change?" Holly realized the question was delving further into his life than he may have cared to go. In which case, he would simply tell her it was off-limits. And that would be that. But since he had opened the line of questioning, she had every right to counter.

"It's a long story," Anderson said.

Holly refused to let him off the hook that easily. "Well, I'm not going anywhere, and since we still have more than two hours of flight time left..."

Anderson chuckled. He understood that if he was curious about her that it only stood to reason that she felt the same about him. After tasting his drink, he turned to her and said, "Fair enough. Back in the day, which was not so long ago, I was a hard-driving, overly ambitious attorney thinking only about my bank account and myself. It played havoc on my personal life and damn near everything else. I finally got smart and decided to try to turn things around. So I changed careers, mellowed out and am the better for it today."

"Good for you," Holly said.

"You'll get no argument from me there."

Holly smiled, but she was still curious about the man. She suspected that his past life also involved a woman, probably a wife.

Sensing that she wanted more, Anderson decided to give it to her. "It cost me a good relationship."

"I'm sorry," she said softly.

"Yeah, so am I. But it happens and we move on."

"Is it really that simple?"

"Sometimes it has to be," he said. "We can't go back. We can only deal with the aftermath and try to avoid past mistakes."

"Yes, I suppose you're right." Holly thought about her own past mistakes where it concerned men. It mainly came down to expecting too much and often receiving too little, which made for a bad mix. She wondered if it might be different were she involved with someone like Anderson. Or was he still damaged goods that she would do well to avoid at all costs?

"So, is there a man waiting for you back in Houston?" Anderson asked, throwing caution to the wind. "Husband, boyfriend, or whatever?" He found it hard to imagine someone like her could be available, but it was worth a try.

"No husband or boyfriend," Holly told him succinctly.

He lifted a brow in surprise. "Is there a story there or…"

"I'm not gay, if that's what you're asking."

"I wasn't," he assured her.

"I've dated, of course," she said. "And I know this sounds like a cliché, but I just haven't found the right man." She couldn't believe she was opening up to this stranger about her love life. Or lack of. But, then again, why not? They would probably never see each other again after the flight. On the plane, though, the close proximity sort of bonded them temporarily.

"That's too bad." *Not really,* he thought. He didn't doubt that such a man existed. She just needed to find him.

"Believe me, I'm not complaining," Holly felt compelled to say. "I'm happy with my life. Besides, these days I'm too busy with work and doing things with my family and friends to be bothered."

Anderson chuckled. "Bothered? Is it really such an imposition on your life to be involved with someone who cares for you?"

Her brows lowered. "I never said it was an imposition."

"You might as well have."

She sighed. "Look, there's more to life than being defined by a relationship. That's all I'm saying. If it happens, it happens. But I won't spend my life looking for something that may never be there. Not when I have so much else to focus on."

"I understand," Anderson said.

"Do you?" Holly asked pointedly.

"Yeah, I do."

She took his word for it, having been judged—or misjudged—all her life in one respect or another. In high school she had been considered too curvy to make the cheerleading squad, but she had made it her goal to prove them wrong. And in college she was thought to be a long shot to be class president. But she had showed them. Even as a journalist she was once thought to be too attractive to be taken seriously. So she had taken on a tough job as a foreign correspondent in Asia and earned her stripes, just to prove them all wrong.

If she ever did hook up with someone, he would have to be able to deal with her independence and career. Not all men could handle that. She wondered which cloth Anderson was cut from in that respect.

"Is there someone waiting for you in Houston?" she asked him. *Might as well find out now, for better or worse.* "Or are you still hung up on that relationship that fell flat?"

Anderson anticipated the last question. It was one that had dogged him for the past two years since his last serious relationship came to an end. Getting over her took time, but he managed to look ahead not behind.

"No, I'm not hung up on her," he said, noticing that their shoulders were touching. "That's water under the bridge, as far as clichés go. And in answer to your other question, no, there's no one waiting for me in Houston."

Holly tried to gauge if there was anything between the lines regarding his availability. Or was he, like her, just living his life while keeping his options open? "Is that by design? Or have you just not found anyone you want to be with?"

"Probably a little of both," he answered honestly.

"Well, good luck either way," she said, lifting her glass to his.

"Back at you." He touched his glass to hers and tasted his drink.

No sooner had Anderson set down his glass than they hit a patch of turbulence that caused the airplane to drop sharply. Holly fell over onto his chest and grabbed hold of him for dear life. Instinctively, he held her in his arms, enjoying the feel of her soft, supple body. The sweet scent of her hair was pleasing to his nostrils. He imagined them together making love in all the wrong places. And even the right ones.

"It's okay," he told her tenderly. "We're not going down."

At that moment, the plane corrected itself and all seemed calm again. Holly, who had seen her life flash before her eyes, realized she was still clinging to Anderson and he seemed in no hurry to release his strong arms from around her.

She sucked in a deep breath, feeling embarrassed that she had let her guard down in a moment of panic. Apparently it was just a false alarm and she would live to see another day. Hopefully many more days.

"I think you can let go of me now," she said.

"No problem." Anderson reluctantly removed his arms. "Just didn't want to do so till I was absolutely sure we were past the danger zone."

Holly leaned back in her seat, wondering what had come over her. Had he been merely a convenient shoulder to lean on? Or was it more about the man himself that made her feel safe in his arms?

She refused to read more into it than it was. Especially since she suspected he was the type that was used to coming to the rescue of damsels in distress, even if he wasn't currently involved with anyone.

"Didn't mean to fall onto you like that," she said self-consciously.

"It wasn't your fault. When you get turbulence like that, none of us can control what happens. I promise not to hold it against you."

"Thank you." He was definitely a perfect gentleman in trying to comfort her, something she didn't take lightly these days. "Guess we should be landing soon."

"Looks like it." In truth, Anderson hated to see the journey come to an end, rough patches and all. He hoped it didn't mean their new acquaintanceship had to end, too.

The plane made a picture-perfect landing at George Bush Intercontinental Airport, and Holly breathed a sigh of relief. Once she stepped into the terminal, she was prepared to put the bumpy ride behind her. She suspected it wouldn't be as easy to forget Anderson.

"I guess this is where we say our goodbyes," he told her as she was about to retrieve her checked luggage.

"I guess it is," she said, forcing herself to smile.

"Actually, it doesn't have to be." Anderson looked down at her. "Maybe we can get together sometime for dinner or whatever."

Holly met his eyes. "You mean like a date?"

"Yeah, a date would be nice." He grinned, hoping it would be enough to win her over for now.

She really had no good reason to say no, other than her normal caution whenever she met anyone new.

"I'm really pretty busy right now…" she began. "But maybe we can get together sometime. Do you have a business card?"

"Of course." Anderson removed a card from his wallet and handed it to her, deciding against pressing his luck at this point. "It has my office and cell phone numbers, along with my email address."

Holly glanced at it, spotting the name Anderson Gunn above his title. She loved the name—it was suave and fit the man. "Thank you." She slipped her hand into her purse and pulled out one of her own business cards. Handing it to him, she said, "If I don't pick up, feel free to leave a message."

"I'll do that," he promised.

She smiled. "Well, I'd better let you get on your way. I'm sure we'll see each other again."

Anderson beamed. "Goodbye, then, Holly."

"Goodbye, Anderson." She watched him walk away and, strangely enough, was already beginning to miss his companionship.

On a sunny afternoon, Holly drove her Subaru Impreza down Interstate 45 toward her father's house, wanting to stop in and say hello before heading to her place. She tried to check in on him as much as possible since her mother died. A proud man, he did his best to try to appear strong and unaffected by much, but she knew he was still hurting after losing his one and only true love.

Will I ever find that type of connection with anyone? she wondered. Or was that something too hard to come by today?

Her mind turned to Anderson. They had gotten off to a rocky start, but seemed to make a connection along the way. But could it go anywhere? Would he actually call her? Should she call him?

Holly turned onto South Wayside Drive and a little later made a right on Wildwood Way. A few houses down, she pulled into the driveway of the redbrick bungalow where she'd grown up. Her father was sitting in his favorite Adirondack chair on the porch, a beer can in his hand.

Robert Kendall was a semiretired dentist. He took part in the free outdoor dental-care clinics offered to low-income residents of the city several times a year. The rest of the time, he enjoyed sports, working on projects around the house and taking long walks.

Holly got out of the car and smiled. "Hey, Dad."

"Hey." His sable eyes crinkled as he smiled.

She stepped onto the porch and gave him a hug.

"How was your trip?"

"Good." She was sure Stuart had already phoned and given him the scoop. "Not counting the turbulence, which was pretty bad a couple of times."

"That's just nature's way of letting you know who's boss."

Holly chuckled. "That's one way of putting it."

"And how are my little granddaughters doing?" Robert asked.

"Full of energy," Holly said. "Why don't you come with me next time and you can see for yourself just how much they've grown."

He took a swig of the beer and shook his head. "They're welcome here anytime. Maybe you should remind your brother of that."

She frowned. "He has a life there, Dad. He can't just leave it behind anytime."

"You seem to do that just fine."

"Maybe I wouldn't if I had to chase two seven-year-olds around all the time."

"He never should've married that gal," Robert said glumly. "She was never good enough for him. Abandoning her daughters like that is unforgivable."

Holly agreed, but there was no point rehashing old news. "The important thing is that Stuart stepped up as a father. Now maybe you should, too, and go visit him and your granddaughters more often."

"Point taken." He drank more beer. "Can I get you something?"

"I'm fine." She sat in the chair that her mother used to occupy and felt a little sad.

"Yeah, I miss her, too," Robert said intuitively.

"I know you do," she said sorrowfully. "It's still hard to believe Momma's gone."

"Yep. Time can only do so much to heal the wounds."

Holly had considered her mother to be her best friend and someone to whom she could talk about anything.

Now she would never get to see what life had in store for her daughter.

"She'd want you to get more out of life," Holly said.

"I'm getting plenty out of life," he insisted.

"What about companionship?" She had not really gone down this path with him before. But, since he'd been a widower for five years, maybe it was time he looked for someone else to spend his time with.

"What about it?" he asked.

"Momma wouldn't want you to be all alone."

"Actually, your momma wouldn't want *you* to be alone," Robert said bluntly. "I'm sixty-three years old and past the stage where I need someone in that way. But you're still young and still single. Maybe it's time *you* let someone in."

Holly thought that was pretty slick of him to turn the tables so it was all about her. She decided to take the bait. "I'm not afraid to do that."

"Could've fooled me."

"Yes, I'm picky, but if he comes along I'll know it—and so will you."

He chuckled coarsely. "Okay, just don't keep me waiting too long. I won't be around forever."

"Don't be too sure about that," she countered. "I have a feeling you've got plenty of gas in the tank and will be there for as many grandchildren as you can handle."

His eyes widened. "You mean there could be more?"

Holly immediately regretted saying that. Yes, she wanted kids, but had no way of knowing if that would ever happen for her. First she had to find a man she liked well enough to become a potential father to her children. Then he had to want kids, too.

Anderson Gunn popped into her head.

Chapter 3

Holly lived in a cul-de-sac in the River Oaks section of Houston, between the downtown and uptown districts. Her modern ranch-style home had hardwood floors, granite countertops, plenty of windows—everything she had wanted. She also had a home office and work-out room, though she preferred to exercise outside, jogging and riding her bicycle.

After putting her things away and catching up on mail and email, she showered and dressed before heading out to meet her friend Madison Wagner for cocktails. The two had met a few weeks ago at a book fair and hit it off.

When Holly walked into the Blue Café, she immediately spotted Madison. She was hard to miss with her long, curly brown hair with blond highlights, gold-flecked brown eyes, beautiful caramel skin tone and an enviously slender frame that Holly would kill to have. As usual, Madison was smartly dressed in designer clothes.

"Hey," Holly said as she approached her.

"Hey, girl." Madison flashed a smile. "Thanks for coming."

"Had to get your take on the hottest books," Holly said. Madison was a successful book reviewer and was known for being brutally honest in her reviews.

"I'll be happy to share. Let's find a place to sit."

Though the place was crowded, they found a table near the back and ordered drinks.

"So how's that good-looking brother of yours doing?" Madison asked.

Though they had never met face-to-face, Madison and Stuart had video chatted one day.

"Busy as ever with work and playing daddy," Holly told her.

"Good for him. Honestly, I've never been the mommy type, but I applaud any single parent who can balance everything in life as he seems to be doing."

Holly had assumed that Madison was cool with children, but apparently not. So much for any possibility of Madison and Stuart getting together someday. Not that she could pass judgment, considering children were not exactly a priority in her own busy life these days. Though not having a man made the idea of being a mother that much harder to grasp.

"It can be very challenging at times," Holly said. "But somehow he manages to get by."

"Don't we all, no matter our challenges."

"True."

A young couple who couldn't seem to keep their hands off each other got up from the table beside theirs. Holly couldn't help but notice the enormous wedding ring on the woman's finger.

"Did you get a load of her ring?" she asked.

Madison smirked. "How could I not?"

Holly sensed that she had hit a sore spot. "What?"

"Two years ago I was engaged. Then my asshole fiancé called the wedding off a week before we were supposed to walk down the aisle."

"You're joking?" Holly asked, though it was evident by the anger in Madison's face that she was anything but playing around.

"I wish I were. It was a terrible time in my life and it still hurts."

"That's awful. I'm sorry. You should've told me before now."

"It's not exactly the way I wanted to begin a new friendship, by sulking over my ex," Madison said. "Especially when I'm trying to move on and forget him, hard as it has been to do."

"I understand." In truth, Holly couldn't imagine falling for someone only to have the rug ripped out from beneath her because he got cold feet or whatever.

"Sorry about that," Madison said. "I didn't mean for tonight to be a downer."

"If I'd known, I never would've gawked over that ring," Holly told her, feeling a little guilty.

"Really, it's fine," Madison assured her. "Just because I was hurt by a jerk doesn't mean you're not entitled to picturing a man slipping a ring on your finger someday."

Holly envisioned that for just a moment, but it still seemed so far away.

Besides, right now this was about Madison, not her.

"I hope you don't let that jerk keep you from giving your heart to another man," Holly said sympathetically.

"I don't want to," Madison said, lifting her drink. "But it is what it is. After putting everything I had into that relationship only to get burned, I'm not ready to get back into the dating game. Maybe someday."

Holly figured this probably wasn't the best time to talk about her own romantic prospects. Especially since she didn't have too many prospects lately.

"Let's talk about books," she said, changing to a more agreeable subject. "I just finished a thriller by Zolton Elliot. It was pretty intense and I would definitely recommend the book, even though the protagonist was a little too perfect. What should I try next?"

Madison tossed back her hair, smiling. "I'm so glad you asked. I can recommend several books and you can pick which one sounds most enticing."

Holly typed in the recommendations on her iPhone, hoping to read them all eventually. They ordered a second cocktail.

* * *

On Saturday morning, Anderson watched the large television screen above the elliptical machine as he worked out at the fitness center. Holly's lovely face was on display as she delivered the news with the professionalism and anchor voice that showed she was in her true element. Since they had said their goodbyes five days ago, he hadn't been able to get the lady out of his mind. Indeed, the only reason he hadn't already called her was that he wanted to allow a few days to pass before asking her out. And maybe a small part of him wanted to give both of them some time to allow their initial meeting to settle in. After his workout, he showered and dressed. He headed outside, squinted in the sunlight and got out his cell phone, dialing Holly's number. She picked up midway through the second ring.

"Hey there, this is Anderson," he said.

"Hi," she said softly.

"Saw you on the news this morning."

"Did you?" She paused. "How did I do?"

"Need you ask?" he responded. "You were great."

"So great that you thought I was on another station."

Anderson chuckled. "And you won't let me forget, will you?"

"Not a chance," she said with a laugh.

"Maybe I can make it up to you," he said. "What are you doing for lunch?"

"Hmm…actually, I already had other plans for lunch. Sorry."

So was he. Might those plans include another man?

Not that he would be scared off by a little competition, but if that were the case, he wanted to know up front.

"It's cool," he said.

"In case you're wondering, I'm meeting with a female colleague to talk shop."

Anderson grinned and felt foolish for being jealous without cause.

"Are you available for dinner?" he asked hopefully.

"Yes, I am," she replied.

He preferred to pick her up, but suspected that might not be to her liking for a first date. "Do you know where the Rooster Place is?"

"Yes, I've been there before."

"How about we meet there at seven?" he asked.

"Seven it is," Holly told him.

"Great. See you then."

After disconnecting, Anderson headed for his silver Mercedes in the parking lot. He was excited at the prospect of going out with Holly, and that was a feeling he hadn't had for a woman in a long time. She had a lot of qualities he admired. He hoped to uncover the rest of her along the way.

Holly was glad to hear from Anderson. In fact, had he not called today, she would have taken the initiative and asked him out. Though she was used to being pursued, this was the twenty-first century and there was absolutely nothing wrong with a woman asking a man out—especially if that man was interesting and easy on the eyes.

Besides, it was nice to forget she was an anchor-woman and let her hair down. Anderson Gunn seemed like a man she could do that with. She looked forward to having dinner with him tonight and learning more about what made him tick, besides work and the sports section.

She drove to the Wine Factory, a trendy café on Uptown Park Boulevard, where she was meeting her friend and fellow anchor at a rival network, Blythe Cramer, for lunch.

They arrived at the same time and gave each other a hug.

"Great tan," Holly said, knowing Blythe had just returned from Hawaii.

"Thanks." She ran a hand through her short blond hair. "I probably spent way too much time in the sun and water in Maui, but what's a girl to do while vacationing in paradise?"

"As long as you had a good time, what more could you ask for?"

"My sentiments exactly," Blythe said. "Let's go taste some wine." A few minutes later they were sitting down, sipping chardonnay and listening to live music by a flamenco guitarist.

"This music is beautiful," Holly said. She immediately found herself wondering what type of music Anderson enjoyed. She pictured him as a classic R&B or urban music lover.

"Yes, it is," seconded Blythe. "But I still have Ha-

waiian music in my head. It will probably take a while
to get past it."

Holly had never been to Maui and was envious of
anyone who had. But unlike Blythe, who was recently
divorced and happy to venture there on her own, she
preferred to take that type of romantic trip with a man.
Maybe one day she would.

"I heard that Bill Togin is retiring when his contract
runs out next month," Blythe told her. "That means
there will be an opening on the coveted evening news."

"Are you going for it?" Holly asked.

"What do you think?"

"That would be a yes," Holly said, smiling.

"You bet it is. I've waited long enough," Blythe said.

"Good luck. I'm not against switching around if the
opportunity presents itself, but for now I love working weekends and having the week to do other things
I enjoy."

"I'd love to do weekends only, if I could afford it,"
Blythe said. "But with my mortgage and credit cards
maxed, I need all the airtime I can muster."

If Holly hadn't known better, she would think that
Blythe was holding it against her that she had been left
a small inheritance by her grandparents a few years
back, much of which she had invested. It allowed her the
luxury of working part-time without falling into debt.

"Who is that hunk?" Blythe suddenly asked, getting
Holly's attention.

Holly turned and her eyes widened when she saw
Anderson enter the room with a tall, gorgeous woman.

* * *

Anderson practically froze when he laid eyes on Holly. She was sitting with an attractive blonde and seemed less than pleased to see him there. Or was it more about who he was with? He looked at his client, Suzy Dillman, whom he had no romantic interest in whatsoever. He suspected Holly might have thought otherwise.

"Will you excuse me for a moment?" he asked Suzy.

"Sure," she responded. "I'll find a table."

"Thanks." Anderson made his way over to Holly, smiling as he walked toward her. "Hello."

"Hey." Holly tried to keep her voice even, though she was beginning to wonder if he was a player or what.

"Do you two know each other?" Blythe asked.

"Yes," Holly said. "This is Anderson Gunn. We met on a plane the other day."

Blythe grinned mischievously. "Well, hello. I'm Blythe Cramer."

"Hi." Anderson eyed Holly again. "Are we still on for dinner tonight?"

"You tell me." She batted her lashes. "Who's your friend?"

He glanced in Suzy's direction and saw that she was waiting patiently. "She's a client and senior partner at Dillman, Benson and Krieg," he explained. "Nothing more."

Holly took him at his word, not wanting to make a big deal out of the fact that his client was an attractive woman. He was entitled to have any clients he wanted without her getting jealous—especially since they hadn't even had their first date yet.

Her lips curved into a smile. "I guess I'll see you then at the Rooster Place."

He smiled back. "I guess you will. Catch you later, and nice meeting you, Blythe."

"You too," she said. She waited till he walked away before turning toward Holly. "Are those sexual vibes I'm picking up between you and Mr. Good-Looking?"

Holly colored. "Right now it's more like getting-to-know-you vibes."

"So the interest is there?"

"Yes," Holly admitted. "We'll see where it goes."

"I hope it goes all the way," Blythe said. "Good men are so hard to find these days."

"Tell me about it." Holly hadn't exactly been looking for men, good or bad, but knew there were some real jerks out there. So far that didn't seem to be the case with Anderson, even if she had jumped the gun in assuming that he had simply found someone else to take on a lunch date that day. Obviously, the man had scruples and was truly interested in seeing if they could start something.

Chapter 4

Holly normally had no trouble deciding what to wear from her vast wardrobe, as she loved to buy new clothes. It was one of her weaknesses and passions. But, in this case, she didn't want to overdress or underdress for her date with Anderson. She had never seen him in anything but an expensive suit and she knew that the attire at the Rooster Place was a few notches above casual, so she chose a three-quarter sleeve paisley print dress and sandals. She brushed her hair into place, dabbed on a little perfume and was on her way.

I'll just play it cool and see how things go, she thought during the drive. If this was meant to go somewhere, it would. If not, then she'd simply get back to her busy life and not worry about it.

She parked in the lot and went inside the restaurant. Anderson walked up to her, spotting her before she had seen him.

"Hi," he said, offering her a handsome smile.

"Hello." She gave him the once-over and liked what she saw. He wore a brown blazer over an orange twill shirt, dark slacks and loafers. He had an obviously fit and trim body, and she would bet that he'd look just as amazing in a T-shirt and athletic shorts.

"Right on time," he said.

"Of course."

"Shall we go in?"

Anderson allowed Holly to lead the way. As with the previous times he had seen her, she was flat-out gorgeous. He liked the dress, too, but imagined he would like it even better if she were wearing nothing at all.

They were seated and handed menus, then they both settled for the prime-rib special and red wine.

Now that he had her all to himself, Anderson wasn't sure where to begin. Though he had gone on a few dates recently, he was admittedly out of practice when it came to being with someone who truly captured his attention. He wanted to do this right.

"Tell me about your family," he said. It seemed a reasonable place to start to get beyond their airplane conversation. He assumed there was more to the family than a brother and nieces.

"Well, you know I have a brother. My dad lives in Houston. He's retired, though sometimes it seems like he works even harder now. I lost my mother to a heart attack a few years ago. No other siblings."

"Sorry to hear about your mother," Anderson said.

"She was such a great lady," Holly said. "I think about her every day."

"I'm sure you do."

She tasted her wine. "Are your parents here?"

His eyes lowered. "I was raised mostly by my mother before she died. Then I was shuffled back and forth between relatives. Never knew my father."

"When did your mother die?" Holly wondered, wishing they didn't have that in common.

"A long time ago," Anderson muttered. "I was nine."

Holly couldn't imagine having lost her mother at such a young age. She was sure it was difficult for him, especially since his father wasn't in the picture.

"Have you ever had any interest in seeing if you could track down your father?" she asked.

"Not really," he said thoughtfully. "What would be the point? I'm not even sure he knows I'm alive. If he does, there's been no attempt to contact me."

"I can't blame you for being put out at the thought. But with your mother no longer here, maybe your dad could somehow compensate for her loss."

Anderson's nostrils flared. Why was she pushing this? "As I said, not interested. Just because you have a father in your life doesn't mean that I need one—especially at this stage."

"I'm sorry." She resented that it seemed to irk him that she had a relationship with her father and he did not, none of which was her doing. Maybe she should have just kept her mouth shut. But then again, why should she? Weren't they here to get to know each other? "Yes, I have a dad who's always there for me. And maybe as a result, I believe that having a connection with a living parent is important—even if it means reaching out to someone who wasn't there for you, perhaps for reasons you were never told. I'm sorry if I overstepped my bounds."

Anderson sucked in a deep breath, knowing he had overreacted. It certainly wasn't the way he had envisioned them bonding. He knew only what his mother had told him about his father, which was virtually next to nothing. She'd only mentioned a one-night stand that left her pregnant and that his father had been out of the picture.

"Don't worry about it," he said to Holly. "I didn't mean to get upset. Who knows, someday I may track down my father, if he's still around, and get his take on things."

She smiled softly. "There's always hope that something good could come out of having an open mind," she said.

"Something already has." Anderson met her eyes. "I'm on a date with a beautiful woman."

She blushed. "Other than that, silly."

"Well, let's just say you've opened my eyes to endless possibilities."

Holly felt the power of his gaze, making it impossible

to deny their sexual attraction. "I'm all about opening one's eyes," she said.

Anderson lifted his glass to that.

After the food had been served, Anderson found himself enjoying watching Holly eat. He wondered what it would be like to feed each other. And much more than just food—kisses and other affectionate gestures, too.

"So, do you always wine and dine gorgeous clients?" Holly asked, seeking a reaction as she nibbled on some lettuce.

"Not always," Anderson promised. "And none of them could hold a candle to you."

"Oh really? I'm supposed to believe that?"

He smiled. "Maybe you don't realize just how hot you are."

She colored, finding it hard not to simply accept his compliments. "Maybe I don't."

"I'll try my best to help you recognize that," he said. "And, just for the record, my client that you saw this afternoon is happily married."

"That's nice to know," Holly admitted. Though she knew some men had no qualms about having an affair with a married woman, she didn't believe Anderson was one of them.

Anderson took that as his cue to move on. "So what are your interests in life?"

"I have lots of them," she said, dabbing a cloth napkin to the corners of her lips. "I love to travel when I have the time, bicycle, attend sports events, dance, go to the theater, listen to classical, jazz and soul music and read fiction. I also enjoy my volunteer work, where I read to children to help increase literacy."

"That all sounds great," he said, impressed. "Certainly seems like your plate is full right now." He wondered if that meant that she wouldn't have time for a serious relationship with anyone.

"Whose isn't full these days?" Holly bit into a slice of bread. "I'm sure you have a fair amount on your plate, too."

"I suppose I do," Anderson conceded. "I also enjoy traveling, fishing, working out at the gym, multiple sports, movies from the forties and fifties and just hanging out with friends."

"That sounds nice, and well-rounded," she told him.

"I'm a well-rounded guy," he said with a chuckle.

She smiled. "What type of music do you like?"

"Classic R&B, urban and a little jazz vocal."

"I knew it," she said. "At least, the first two."

He put a hand to his chin. "So you think you have me all figured out, huh?"

"I don't know about that, but at least the music."

"A good start," he said. "I'll be happy to fill in the blanks whenever you like."

"Good. I plan to hold you to that," she promised.

At the moment, he would have just settled for holding her. The thought of their bodies touching had a rippling effect through Anderson, causing his temperature to rise. Was she feeling the vibe, too?

After the meal, Anderson walked Holly to her car.

He wanted more than anything to kiss her. Something told him she felt the same.

He leaned in slowly and grazed her lips.

Holly felt his lips on hers and was quick to reciprocate. She had been hoping Anderson would kiss her, as it seemed the perfect way to end what had been a pleasant date. The kiss, which lasted for several scintillating seconds, wasn't a disappointment in the slightest. She liked that he wasn't pushing for too much, too soon, and was respectful in giving them both something to look forward to the next time.

In her mind, it was a given that there would be a next time. But were they on the same wavelength?

The following Wednesday, Holly rode her bicycle to the nearby park, taking advantage of its bicycle-friendly paths. She meant to ask Anderson if he bicycled. Somehow she couldn't imagine that he didn't or wouldn't want to if she invited him to ride with her sometime.

In the afternoon, she went to the McCawlin Elementary School, where she spent over an hour reading to children at different grade levels. The kids always loved her visits. Her volunteer work was special to her because as a child she had benefited from volunteer readers to improve her own reading skills.

By the time Holly got home, she was ready for a nice hot bath. While running the water, she allowed herself to fantasize about what it would be like to make love to Anderson. She pictured him as a gentle but thorough lover and one who probably couldn't get enough of whatever woman he set his sights on.

Calm down, girl, she told herself, feeling the heat on her skin as she allowed her mind to wander to uncharted but desirable territory. It had clearly been too long since she had been wined, dined and kissed by a man, and she enjoyed it.

But that didn't mean she had to get too carried away with the early stages of a romance. They had a long way to go before it was the real deal for both of them.

On the other hand, it did no harm to let her imagination have a little fun, even if it had yet to mesh with reality.

Something told her, though, that if things continued between them it was only a matter of time before things progressed to the next level.

She climbed into the bathtub and let the bubbly warm water do its work.

On Friday, Anderson dropped by the lakefront home of his close friend and fellow lawyer, Lester Powell. The two had attended law school together. Anderson had been Lester's best man at his first wedding, but was out of town when he'd walked down the aisle the second time.

They sat on the patio, talking and drinking beer.

"You've got that look," Lester said. He had long black Rastafarian locks that bordered a thin face with a goatee.

"What look might that be?" Anderson asked, dumbfounded.

"The look that tells me you're getting some, or you're about to."

Anderson laughed and gulped down beer from the bottle. "Since when did you become so insightful?"

"Since our college days, when I watched your ass coming and going with one chick after another."

That got another laugh out of Anderson. "I think you're talking about yourself." He had always been a one-woman man for all of college. The fact that he hadn't been able to keep the relationships going was another matter, and he blamed it on a combination of immaturity and a sometimes misguided sense of direction.

But times had changed. Or at least he had.

"So tell me who's got you all hot and bothered these days?" Lester pressed.

Anderson sat back and took another drink. "Her name is Holly. She's an anchor at KOEN."

"Anchorwoman, huh? Where did you meet her?"

"At the airport in Portland, believe it or not."

Lester grinned. "I can believe it, though every lady I've ever met at the airport was either old enough to be my mother or had a man who kept her on a short leash."

"I think you've done all right for yourself in the romance department," Anderson said. Lester's latest marriage to a sweet professor seemed to be working.

"Yeah, I guess I have." Lester lifted his bottle. "Just how serious are things with this Holly?"

"Not too serious at the moment," Anderson said honestly. "We're just beginning to feel our way. I think I might have found someone I can really relate to."

"More power to you. Can't wait to meet her."

"You can check her out weekend mornings on KOEN and let me know what you think," Anderson said.

"You bet." Lester studied him. "So have you totally gotten you-know-who out of your system?"

Anderson looked away thoughtfully. "Yeah, she was out of my system a long time ago."

"You sure about that?"

"I'm very sure. We both moved on and there's no looking back. I'm happy about where I am today."

"Glad to hear that," Lester said. "You know I've got your back and want you to be as happy with someone as I am."

"I know." Anderson smiled while tasting the beer. "I'm working on that."

He thought about Holly and couldn't help but feel that she was his future if he had any say in the matter. And he did. He just had to see how things would play out and then Holly would be his.

Chapter 5

On Sunday morning, Holly did the newscast, reporting the local and national news of interest. When she
was done, she left the set and was met by the station
manager, Felix Yasmin, who was fiftysomething and
thickset.

"Good going," he said.

She was used to receiving a positive review of her
anchoring, but always tried to read between the lines to
see if there was anything she could do better.

"Thanks," she said. "That story on the missing new-
lywed was scary. I hope he shows up alive and well."

"Yeah, we all do." Felix paused. "Do you have a moment?"

"Sure."

She followed him into his office, feeling tense. What was this about?

"Have a seat," he said.

She sat down in a chair in front of his desk and he sat beside her.

Felix ran a hand through his thinning gray hair. "Look, I know you've settled into the morning slot and we're happy with you there. But I was wondering how you'd feel about moving to the evening spot on weekends?"

"Wow." The last Holly knew, Scott Turner was ensconced in the position. What had changed?

"Scott resigned," Felix informed her before she could ask. "Apparently he took a position with a competing station."

"Sorry to hear that," Holly said, immediately thinking about the opening at KRVA that Blythe had coveted. It looked as though she had been passed over for a man.

"I can't think of anyone more qualified or deserving to take Scott's place than you," Felix said. "So what do you think?"

Holly understood that she did not have the luxury of sitting on this for a while, not with the fast pace and quick turnover in the business. Yes, she loved working mornings, but she would be a fool to pass up the weekend evening news.

"Yes, I'd love to do it," she told him, smiling.

Felix smiled back. "I was hoping you'd say that. There will be a pay raise, of course, and some other little perks that come with the job. You'll start next weekend."

"I can hardly wait." Holly wondered who would take her place on the morning slot.

"Excellent." He stood up. "Well, enjoy the rest of your day."

Once in her car, Holly phoned Blythe, confirming what she had suspected.

"How could they stab me in the back like that?" Blythe cried.

"I know," Holly said. She considered Scott a friend, and knew that he had only taken an opportunity that he was given. "It's a tough business."

"Tell me about it."

"I'm sure another opening will come along," Holly said.

"Yeah, right, and they'll probably pass over me again," Blythe grumbled.

"You don't know that."

"You know something I don't?" Blythe asked.

Holly sighed and decided to share her own news, hoping it didn't further depress Blythe. "I was offered the job that Scott vacated and accepted it."

"I wouldn't have expected any less," Blythe said cheerfully. "Enough pitying myself. Congratulations! And I really mean it."

"Thank you for saying that."

"Us anchor girls have to stick together."

"Always."

Holly drove to her father's place to check on him.

Using her key to get in, she found him asleep in his favorite well-worn recliner. The dishes were piled up in the kitchen, so she put them in the dishwasher, knowing that her mother had once done all the household chores that her father now had to do himself. He hadn't made the adjustment very well thus far and maybe he never would.

Holly wanted to do her part to help whenever she could, even if he was usually resistant to the idea, insisting he could take care of himself.

She heard a sound and turned to see her father standing there, rubbing his eyes. "Didn't hear you come in."

"Not surprised since you were sleeping pretty good there," she said.

"It wasn't necessary to clean up in here," he said, frowning.

"I know, but I wanted to." She smiled. "It's fine."

Robert tilted his head. "When are you going to get a man of your own to clean up after?"

"I already have one," Holly said, half joking. "I don't need two."

"You know what I mean."

She thought about Anderson, but didn't want to tip her hand too soon about something that could turn out to be nothing that lasted. Somehow she did not picture him as the type who left dirty dishes around or otherwise needed a maid. But what did she really know about him at this point?

Gazing at her father, Holly said, "I wish I had a crystal ball to predict my future with a man. Guess we'll both just have to wait and see what happens." She walked over to him and kissed his cheek. "Until then, you'll just have to put up with me."

Robert grinned. "I guess I can manage, if that's how you feel."

"It is." She shared her work news, which he congratulated her on, and then went home.

Holly was watering plants while thinking about Anderson and when they would get together again. In her mind soon was not soon enough.

As though he had mental telepathy, Anderson called her cell phone right then.

"Hey, beautiful," he said.

"Hey, handsome," she responded, not shying away from returning the compliment.

"I was wondering if you were available for a late lunch."

Holly smiled. "Yes, as a matter of fact, I am."

"Good. How about at my place? I make a mean chicken sandwich and great salad."

Holly pondered briefly what it meant to accept an invitation that was not in a neutral setting and finally decided that she was ready to move forward in their relationship.

"I'd love to come."

He gave her the address and she recognized the high-priced area where he lived. The fact that Anderson was successful and could cook, too, was definitely something she could get used to. Holly could only imagine what else might be in store as she got to know even more about this interesting man.

After changing into more comfortable clothing, Holly drove to the Galleria, an upscale development in the city's Uptown District. She pulled into the parking garage and took the elevator up seventeen floors to the penthouse of the luxury high-rise.

Anderson was waiting for her, looking great in a yellow polo shirt and navy khakis. He gave her a kiss on the cheek as if they were old buddies rather than potentially new lovers.

"Hope you didn't have any trouble finding the place," he said.

"None at all."

"Good." Anderson smiled at her. She was a sight for sore eyes in a scoop neck multicolored top and tight jeans. It was all he could do not to take her in his arms at that moment and give her a passionate kiss. But he showed the restraint of a gentleman, not wanting to send the lady running out of there before she could get comfortable in his digs. "How about a tour of the place?" he offered.

"I'd love it," Holly said, following him across the bamboo floor through the spacious condominium. The furnishings were an eclectic mix of antique finished leather and traditional wood, with floor-to-ceiling windows offering magnificent panoramic views of Houston. As she had expected, the place was spotless. "Very nice."

"I saved the best for last," Anderson said as he led

her into the kitchen with a gourmet island, gas cooktop and custom cherrywood cabinetry.

"Mmm…something sure smells good," Holly said as she glanced around the impressive kitchen.

"That would be our lunch." It had been a while since he had put his cooking skills to work for a woman and Anderson was slightly nervous, wanting to impress her.

"Can I help?" Holly asked.

"Yes, you can set the table. Dishes are in that cabinet and silverware in that drawer," he said, pointing. With any luck, she would be around enough to know the place by heart.

"Will do." Holly washed her hands and proceeded to do her part as they worked in unison preparing for lunch. It amazed her just how comfortable she felt in his home, as though they had been seeing each other for a while. That was definitely a good sign.

At the dining room table, Anderson opened the white wine while listening with interest as Holly told him about her job promotion. He didn't doubt that she deserved everything that came her way. Including him.

"I won't even pretend to know the ins and outs of television news," he said, "but I gather that there's an endless stream of material you have to digest and decide what to report."

"That's about the size of it," Holly said, lifting her chicken sandwich. "We try to broadcast what's most relevant and leave it to the competition to do the fluff stories."

"Well, you do a damned good job of it."

"Why, thank you." She couldn't help but smile at the compliment before biting into the sandwich. "I do my best, but I know that I'm far from perfect."

"Could have fooled me," he said, tilting his head while studying her. "From this perspective, all I see is perfection."

Holly laughed. "Where do you get your lines from?" She wondered how many other women he had used the lines on.

"I get them from here—" He hit his chest with a balled hand. "I only say what I mean."

"Fine. I'll let you off the hook this time."

"That's good enough for me," he said. "So where have you traveled, other than to Portland?"

"You mean in the United States?"

"There and anywhere else."

"I've been to New York, Los Angeles, Seattle, Detroit, Chicago, Miami and a few other U.S. cities," Holly said. "In addition, I've been to Vancouver, British Columbia, London and Nigeria."

"You have traveled a lot," Anderson remarked. "Why Nigeria in particular versus some other country in Africa?"

"Good question." She wiped her mouth with a napkin. "I went there when I was in college. A dorm friend was from Lagos and she invited me to visit. I figured why not?"

He nodded. Apparently a little fear of turbulence did not stop her from flying quite a bit, which was good.

"What about you? Where have you traveled in and

out of the country?" Holly asked, sipping wine. She imagined he had probably been to quite a few places.

"I've pretty much been to all of the big cities in the continental United States at one time or another," Anderson admitted. "I also went to Honolulu once—beautiful landscape."

"Lucky you." Holly thought about Blythe's recent trip to Hawaii, which made her feel left out of the supposedly breathtaking experience. "Where else?"

"Mexico City, Toronto, the Bahamas, and I've also visited London, Paris and Switzerland."

"Wow, that's impressive."

"No more than your travels," he said.

"So were these trips abroad romantic outings?" Holly asked, as they made their way to the great room and looked out the window. She was envious of the women who may have accompanied him.

Anderson hadn't expected the question but didn't want to dodge it. "They were mostly business trips," he said. "But I did go to Paris with someone years ago."

"Was it the one you let get away?" she wondered, remembering the relationship he had lost.

"No, it was someone else," he said. "We went there on business and it became something more, but fizzled quickly. We both ended up regretting it."

"Do you always get into relationships that end quickly or prematurely?" she asked. Now was probably a good time to know, she thought.

Anderson supposed he deserved that, all things considered. He gazed into her eyes. "No," he promised.

"It's certainly not what I want out of this budding relationship."

"Are you sure about that?"

"As sure as I've felt about anything." The last thing he wanted was for her to believe he was afraid of commitment.

"Just wondering before either of us gets too deep into this."

"Deep works for me," Anderson said, facing her.

"Me too," Holly said, looking up into his eyes. "As long as we're always honest with each other every step of the way."

"Agreed. Scout's honor."

"Were you a Scout?" she asked.

"Cub and Boy Scout," he said proudly. "I learned a thing or two."

She chuckled. "Not sure I want to know what it was."

"Only how to take responsibility for one's actions and how to fasten a tie."

"Oh, well, both of those sound very practical."

"They were." Anderson regarded her in earnest, holding her shoulders. "There is one thing I didn't learn in my Scout days…"

"What might that be?"

"This—"

He angled his head and kissed her. She opened her mouth slightly so their lips aligned perfectly.

Anderson pulled Holly closer to his body so he could feel the contours of hers. He inhaled the scent of her perfume, which made him feel even hotter. He turned his face to the other side to enjoy the power of her kiss from a different angle.

Holly was breathless from the kiss that also left her seeing stars. She had always believed that a man's kiss could make or break any possible relationship. In this case, Anderson's kiss was definitely making the case for a sustained relationship between them. She opened her mouth wider, prompting him to do the same as they moved more deeply into the kiss, arousing her from head to toe. She imagined how fulfilling it would be if and when they made love.

The kiss went on unabated in its intensity. Holly felt warm and moist all over, something she couldn't remember feeling to this degree from a kiss. It left her breathless and wanting more.

But she also wanted things to move along at a gradual pace so that they could enjoy the slow torture of seduction every step of the way.

It was with that thought in mind that she forced herself to break away from his lips. Her eyes lifted to Anderson's. "That was really nice, but I think we need to slow down just a little."

Anderson could barely contain his desire for her. But, given his past experiences with moving too fast only to see things fizzle, he was inclined to agree with her.

"I understand," he said, smiling.

Holly touched her swollen lips, feeling as though he was still kissing them passionately. "Thank you."

"Thank *you*," Anderson countered, "for coming into my life and giving us a chance at something special."

"I could say the same about you. We'll see where this goes, but I am certainly enjoying it so far."

To prove it, Holly gave him one more quick kiss before turning and walking out of his loft.

Chapter 6

Two weeks later, Holly went jogging with Madison. She was barely able to keep up with her friend, who was in excellent shape. She confided in Madison that she was seeing a man, and she hoped it wouldn't somehow bring back memories of Madison's own disastrous relationship.

"How long?" Madison asked.

"Not long," Holly told her, though it seemed like she had known Anderson forever.

"I'm happy for you."

Holly took a breath. "Really?"

Madison looked at her. "Of course. Why wouldn't I be?"

"I just thought—" Holly fumbled for the right words.

Madison frowned. "You thought that because my ex-fiancé turned out to be a jerk, I wouldn't want any of my friends to date someone who could make them happy? Give me more credit than that."

"I'm sorry." Holly wiped perspiration from her brow. "It's just that I've never known anyone who actually had her wedding called off. I wasn't sure where to go with that."

"It's okay," Madison said. "If I were in your shoes, I guess I wouldn't be sure how you'd react either. So what does he do for a living?"

"He's a legal consultant," Holly said. "And a successful one at that."

"That's always a plus."

"I didn't go looking for that, but it is nice that he's gainfully employed, not to mention devilishly handsome."

Madison chuckled. "Those certainly help."

Holly laughed. "That's for sure."

"And I suppose he's dynamite in bed, too?"

Holly colored. "I wouldn't know. We haven't had sex yet."

"Your choice or his?"

"Both. We're taking it slow, going with the flow and all that."

Madison twisted her lips. "Good idea. Maybe if I had done that with my ex instead of jumping in the sack on our second date, I would've seen him for what he truly was and gotten the hell out of the relationship before he hurt me."

Holly truly felt for her. Obviously Madison still had a chip on her shoulder that was preventing her from moving on.

"Do you still love him?" Holly had to ask.

"Hell no!" Madison insisted. "Been there, done that. Trust me when I say I'm over him."

Holly had her doubts about that, but would take her word for it. "So maybe it's time you found someone to share your life."

"You know, maybe you're right," Madison said. "I'll try to keep an open mind from now on and see if Mr. Really Right comes my way."

"You know what they say—hope springs eternal," Holly said.

"Yeah, right," Madison said. "For now, I'd rather hear all about your new man."

"There's not much more to tell right now, other than he's never been married, has no children and travels a lot with his job. He also seems to be crazy about me."

Madison smiled. "And you feel the same way about him?"

Holly blushed. "Well, he has brought a spark into my life, and we do seem to get along so far. As for being crazy about him, I'll hold off on that till things begin to heat up a bit."

"Got it," Madison said. "Great sex can certainly do wonders for making a person a little crazy about someone else. Not that I know anything about that from recent memory."

"So now you can begin to create new memories," she said optimistically.

"Hey, I'm still a long way from where you are now, but I'm all for brand-new memories and tossing the old ones in the trash."

Holly smiled. "Sounds good to me."

"So when do I get to meet your consultant man?" Madison asked.

"Soon," Holly promised as she began to feel strain on her leg muscles. "Right now, I just want to continue to work on what we have before I start introducing him to my friends." Not that she believed for one moment that it would jinx the relationship. It was more that she wanted to feel confident things between her and Anderson were truly the real deal before she got too carried away with introducing him to everyone in her life.

They ran up a hill and down, and then sprinted through the park before beginning their cooldown.

On a Wednesday afternoon, Anderson headed toward the soup kitchen on Mission Avenue. As part of the new-and-improved man he had become, over the past couple of years he had given his time once a month as a volunteer to help feed the needy. After a smart investment had paid off, he had even anonymously paid off their mortgage to allow them to stay afloat. He knew his mother would have approved, had she lived long enough to see it.

He was only too happy to give something back to the

community, since he felt he had certainly been blessed more often than not.

That had certainly been the case since he'd met Holly. They seemed to connect intellectually and, most of all, romantically. And she was doing a lot to help him discover romance again. This time, he planned to do it right because he had no intention of losing her.

He had told her about the soup kitchen and she had quickly offered to accompany him there sometime. In turn, he had agreed to participate in the school literacy program that she was devoted to.

Stepping inside the redbrick building, Anderson immediately laid eyes on Esther Wright, the woman who ran the soup kitchen. She had once been homeless and a drug addict, but she had cleaned herself up and made something of her life.

"Afternoon, Anderson," Esther said with a big smile. "Nice to see you, as always."

"You too, Ms. Wright," he said, smiling at the forty-something woman.

"You all set to work?"

"Ready as ever," he assured her.

"That's what I like to hear," she said. "We can always use your help."

A couple of minutes later, Anderson had put on an apron, hairnet and gloves and stood beside Esther, serving candied yams and brown rice. He would bring Holly the next time—he was sure she would light up the sometimes gloomy place with her beautiful smile and engaging personality.

"I think it's time you got yourself a girlfriend," Esther told him. "You can't let some past mistakes weigh you down forever."

Anderson cracked a smile. One time when he had been feeling down, he had told her about some things he wasn't particularly proud of from his past, such as ending a relationship the wrong way and wishing he could go back and do things differently.

Instead of passing judgment on him, she had literally taken him by the hand and made him feel that burying his head wasn't the way to go, but that he instead should take whatever he could from a bad situation and turn it into a positive. He had done just that by being a lot less self-centered and by volunteering to help those in need.

"I hear you," he told Esther thoughtfully. "As a matter of fact, I'm seeing someone now. Her name is Holly and I plan to bring her here soon so you can meet her."

Esther's brown eyes lit up. "That would be wonderful. I'm so happy for you."

"Thanks. You'll like her."

Anderson doubted that anyone could like Holly more than he did, though. She had the energy to keep up with him and the passion to succeed in her field while still finding time for the new man in her life.

He missed her whenever they were apart. Maybe he could do something about that.

The next day, Anderson was sitting at the desk in his office. He placed a call to the station manager at KOEN and offered his services as a legal consultant. The majority of his work came through referrals and contacts he'd built up during his days as a corporate attorney. But, in this instance, he hoped that putting himself out there might be a way to better acquaint himself with Holly's world. And, in turn, he could get to know her better as a businesswoman.

The manager, Felix Yasmin, seemed enthusiastic and agreed to meet with him this afternoon.

Since Holly worked weekends, Anderson felt there was little chance they would bump into each other. If things went as planned, he would surprise her. If not, she need never be the wiser that he had tried to add the station to his client list.

By two o'clock, Anderson was in Felix Yasmin's small office, exchanging handshakes with the shorter, stockier man and the station's taller, thinner lawyer, Blair Fisher.

"Your résumé is impressive," Felix said as they all sat down. "As are your references."

"It comes with being around for a while."

"Looks like you've made the most of it," Blair said. "I'm curious. With your impressive qualifications, why the interest in this station in particular?"

Anderson suspected he would ask that and had prepared an answer. "I like your programming, plain and simple," he told them. "Especially the news. You seem right on top of the latest happenings and present it very professionally. Seemed like a great place to lend my expertise on legal matters."

"Great answer," Felix said. "I think we could make

good use of your talents in dealing with some of the issues we face."

Anderson grinned as he shook hands with the men. He looked forward to springing the news on Holly when they got together tonight for dinner at the Aspen Club.

Ten minutes later, he left the office with Felix and was about to head out when they ran into Holly.

"Hey," Anderson said evenly. He hadn't expected to see her there today.

"Hey." Holly lifted a brow, surprised to find him there. She was even more taken aback to see him with Felix. "What are you doing here?"

Anderson was about to respond when Felix asked, "Do you two know each other?"

"Yes, we're friends," Anderson said, seeing no reason to divulge the personal nature of their relationship. "Isn't this your off day?"

"I often come in on 'off days' to prepare stories," she told him. "The news never takes an off day."

Anderson realized too late that he should have anticipated this.

Holly looked from one man to the other. "Will someone clue me in as to what's going on here?" she asked. Her eyes settled on Anderson.

"Well, I'm—" He stumbled with the words. He hadn't wanted her to find out like this.

"Anderson's our new consultant," Felix said. "He'll be working with our legal department."

"I see…" Holly glared at Anderson. She couldn't believe what she was hearing. Just what did he think he was doing going behind her back to work for the station?

"It's good that he already knows someone here. It will make the transition that much easier." Felix looked at Holly. "Why don't you show Anderson around?"

"I'd be happy to," she mustered. He had some explaining to do. She waited till they were alone before confronting him. "Why the hell did you decide to work for KOEN?"

Anderson cocked a brow. Clearly she was pissed, though he wasn't quite sure why. It wasn't as if he had stepped on someone's toes. Or had he? "Actually, I'm not an employee of the station, technically speaking."

"Don't patronize me," she said. "You're working with the legal department, whatever you want to call it."

"Okay, okay, whatever." He took a breath. "It's still not what you think."

"So why don't you tell me what it is, then, Anderson?" Holly tried to keep an open mind, but she wasn't comfortable with someone she was involved with also being part of her workplace.

He resisted the urge to give her a hug to calm her down, feeling it wasn't appropriate in the setting. "I offered my services here because I thought it was a nice way to spend more time with you in a professional environment."

"But why?" she asked, trying to wrap her mind around it. "This isn't a game. It's where I work."

"I know," he said, lowering his voice. "I care for you.

We get along well. So why not see if that applies under any circumstances?"

"I'm not sure I understand where you're coming from." She met his eyes. "You don't need to prove to me that we can get along great wherever we are. I already know that."

"So what seems to be the problem?"

Her brows knitted. "First of all, you should have come to me before you came up with this plan, and I would have told you it was a bad idea. Secondly, I have made a habit of never dating anyone I work with. I'm sorry."

Anderson took a moment to collect his thoughts. He had gone about this whole thing the wrong way and had now boxed himself into a corner. He couldn't lose her. Not over this. "I'm sorry," he said in earnest. "You're right, I should have told you my plan. I actually hoped it would please you, not turn you off."

"I'm not turned off," she told him. "I'm being practical. Work and romance simply do not mix, even with the best of intentions. Maybe you've never had a workplace romance."

He peered at her. "And you have?"

"Once, a long time ago," Holly admitted. "It was short and not very sweet. I knew then that I'd never make that mistake again."

"We're not a mistake," Anderson said. "Far from it."

"I feel the same way—as long as we keep our professional and personal lives separate."

"As far as I'm concerned, they are separate," he told

her. "You'll probably never see me around here. Most of the time I do my consulting over the phone or at a restaurant. Nothing has to change between us."

In spite of wanting to believe that, Holly knew she couldn't back down. "Are you saying you're not going to tell Felix you've had a change of heart?"

"I'm not quite sure it's that simple," he said.

"I think it is," she insisted. "I'm sure that if you're honest when you explain things, Felix will understand."

Anderson frowned. "Problem is, I made a commitment to act as a consultant. As a professional, my reputation means as much to me as yours does to you. If I come across as unreliable, it could sully my reputation."

"Maybe you should have thought about that before you came up with this master plan of yours," Holly said sharply. "Or maybe you just don't give a damn what I think."

"You know that's not true," Anderson said.

"I don't know anything, except that we can't be together if we're employed by the same business."

He could see that she had drawn a line in the sand, as had he. "Why don't we go somewhere and talk about this?"

"I think we've already talked enough."

Anderson sighed. "I don't." He reached out for her hand, but she turned away.

"I have some other errands to run, so…" She left it at that, wanting to get out of there before any more words were said that could further strain whatever was left between them.

Minutes later, Holly was driving away and feeling disappointed with Anderson. She had not seen this coming and had really thought they were about to embark on something special. But if he couldn't respect her wishes about her workplace, what type of future could they honestly expect to have?

Chapter 7

Holly was at home watching television—well, more like staring at the screen but having no idea what was on. Her mind was preoccupied with Anderson and wondering if she had gone too far in asking him to terminate his business relationship with the station. It had been more than a week since they had argued about it and neither had called the other. Was it really worth losing what they had simply because he did consulting work for KOEN, supposedly as a means to get closer to her?

Just as she began to have second thoughts about it, Holly wondered if she really needed to lower her principles for a man who seemed to think it was perfectly fine to romance someone in the workplace—even if the romance had come before their professional acquaintance.

If he cared about my feelings at all, he would have asked me first if it was okay for him to be a legal consultant at the station, she thought. *But no, like most men, he did what he wanted to do without thinking about my feelings.*

She was miserable, and he was to blame. Maybe it was better that she had found out now how selfish Anderson could be before she got too deeply involved with him.

Holly's cell phone rang and she hoped it was Anderson. Instead, it was her brother, Stuart, calling.

"Hey, sis," he said cheerfully.

"Hey back. Is everything all right with the girls?"

"Yes, they're fine, other than missing their favorite aunt. What about you?"

"I've had better days," she admitted.

"Want to tell me about it?"

"Not really," she said, folding her legs beneath her on the couch.

"C'mon, that's what big brothers are for. Maybe I can help."

Holly finally decided to let down her wall of resistance and told him about her situation with Anderson and where things now stood.

"I didn't know you were seeing anyone," Stuart said.

"Now you do," she told him. "At least I was. I'm not so sure anymore where this is headed, if anywhere."

"My advice is to stick to your guns," he surprised her by saying. "I think you did the right thing standing up for yourself. If he refused to back down, that's telling you he might not be the right guy for you."

"You think?" In fact, Blythe had suggested the same thing. Holly was confused. She enjoyed Anderson's company and he had been a true gentleman. But then he had to go and break the magical spell by stubbornly refusing to tell Felix he had made a mistake. "I thought all you guys with your superior attitudes stuck together."

Stuart laughed. "Not this time," he said. "Sorry to disappoint you."

"You didn't," she told him. "Just the opposite."

"Look on the bright side—if this dude turns out to be a flake, you can always relocate to Portland and I can introduce you to someone who would worship the ground you walk on."

"Yeah, right." She rolled her eyes. "I don't want anyone to worship me. I want someone who is my equal in a relationship." She had thought that was the case with Anderson, but apparently he was only interested in a relationship on his terms.

"Well put, little sister. Now I know why you're such a great role model for Dottie and Carrie."

Holly was flattered. Her nieces were little angels and deserved much more than they had gotten from their mother. Stuart was great with them, but he could only do so much as a father. She hoped he would find someone soon to share his life with.

She felt better after hanging up. Perhaps it wasn't in her best interest to call Anderson and let him back in her life. Maybe he had moved on in spite of the supposedly deep connection they had between them. So why put herself out there if it wouldn't accomplish anything other than letting him have his way?

Anderson sat at the bar next to his friend Lester, tasting some suds and trying to figure out what went wrong between him and Holly. One moment they were seemingly well on their way to something extraordinary, the next their relationship had stalled for reasons that eluded him. Did she really want to end things simply because he was doing some consulting work for her employer? What was that about?

Moreover, why couldn't he swallow his pride and do the right thing? Wasn't she worth that and a hell of a lot more?

"This is on you," Lester said, getting his attention.

"What's that?" Anderson asked.

"There you are trying to sabotage a relationship again."

"That's not what this is about," Anderson said.

"Isn't it?" Lester's eyes narrowed. "Whenever you let a woman get close, you manage to successfully push her away."

Anderson tasted his beer. "I didn't push her away. It was just the opposite. I tried to get closer, but she shot that down."

"No, you shot it down by putting her in a position where she would have to break her own rules, which were there for a reason," Lester said. "You need to respect the fact that she wants her professional space separate from her personal life. If you had told her up front what you had in mind, she could have stopped you in your tracks. But it didn't work out that way."

"All right, so I screwed up," Anderson conceded. "How do I fix it?"

Lester eyed him hard. "You know how. Tell the station you can't work for them anymore because of a conflict of interest or because you have too heavy a workload, or whatever."

"Then what does that make me—a wimp for giving in?"

Lester laughed. "No, it makes you a *man* for recognizing what's most important in life. In this case, I think it's Holly, if I've read you correctly."

"You have. I want her back in my life."

"So you have your answer," Lester said, lifting his mug. "We both know you don't need the money and that you have consulting gigs left and right. Don't screw up what seems to be a good thing before I even get a chance to meet her."

Anderson grinned. "Yeah, I'll try not to deny you that opportunity."

Was it too late? Yes, it had only been a week since things had stalled between him and Holly. But that could be a lifetime in a relationship. Did she see him as someone who wouldn't bend and, therefore, poor boyfriend material in the long run?

Or, like him, would she view it merely as the type of bump in the road that every relationship experienced at one time or another?

* * *

The next morning, Anderson called Felix Yasmin and told him that he would no longer be able to work for KOEN, citing that he had overextended himself and wouldn't have been able to give them the attention they deserved from a legal consultant.

Felix accepted his decision, but made it clear that if things should change in the future, they would be happy to have him back on their legal team.

Anderson didn't plan to go down that road again. Not when Holly was a much better bet for his future.

He called her and hoped she wouldn't hit the ignore button when she saw his name on the caller ID.

"Hi," she said, answering for a video chat.

"Hi." Anderson was delighted to see her lovely face again. "How have you been?"

"Busy, for the most part," Holly said.

He wondered if that meant too busy to miss him very much. "I wanted to let you know that I'm no longer a consultant for KOEN."

"Really?" Holly was surprised at the news. It had really seemed as if he had dug his heels in for the long run.

"Yeah, it wasn't a good fit," Anderson told her. "But you are."

"Is that so?"

"Yes. I'm sorry if I caused us to fall offtrack. I hope it doesn't mean we can't get back on it."

"I think we can," she said. "And your apology is accepted."

Anderson breathed a sigh of relief. "That's good to know."

"I should probably apologize myself. Maybe I did jump the gun in not wanting you there, but—"

"You don't have to explain," he said. "I understand. It won't happen again. I just want to pick up where we left off and see how things go."

"I'd like that, too," Holly said, smiling.

Anderson grinned. "I've missed you."

"Same here."

"Can I take you out to dinner tonight?"

"Dinner sounds good," she said. "Only this time I'd like to cook you a meal."

"Even better," he said. "But only if I bring the wine."

"Be my guest. Seven-thirty?"

Anderson got her address and could hardly wait to see her in person. This time he was determined not to make the same relationship mistakes he had made before. He would see this through, no matter what was in store.

At six o'clock, Holly did a little more tidying up of her house before preparing the meal. She wanted it to be special. She hadn't cooked for a man other than her father and brother in some time. The menu for the night was breaded veal cutlets, mashed potatoes, greens, corn-bread muffins and peach cobbler. She had learned how to cook these and other foods from her mother, who could make any meal from scratch.

I'm so glad Anderson called, she thought while peeling potatoes. It had been killing her not seeing him, even though it had been her decision. But she had begun to wonder if her reasoning was worth ending a relationship that seemed so full of promise. Also, having Anderson in her life had made Holly aware of the void she had been seeking to fill through her job and volunteer work. She understood now how much she had really missed male companionship.

Especially in the form of Anderson Gunn.

While the food was cooking, she got ready for her dinner date, slipping into a mulberry-colored halter cocktail dress and matching sandals. She pulled her hair back with clips and splashed a touch of perfume along her neckline and on each wrist.

When seven-thirty rolled around, the food was ready and so was Holly.

The doorbell rang right on cue and Holly peeked out and saw Anderson standing there. She took a sweeping glance at her house, as if she could change anything that wasn't quite right at this point, before opening the door.

"Hi," Anderson said, grinning.

"Hey." Holly returned the smile. "Did you find it all right?"

"Sure did. I have GPS in my car, so it practically drives itself anywhere I want to go."

"Must be nice."

"Yeah, it is. But not half as nice as you look tonight."

"Thank you." She beamed.

Holly showed him in. She closed the door and faced her guest, who looked spiffy in a black shirt and taupe pants. His head was freshly shaved and he was holding a bottle of red wine.

"I hope this will do," Anderson said, handing her the bottle of cabernet sauvignon.

"I think it will do just fine," Holly said, smiling at him.

"Great house you've got here."

"I like it," she admitted. "It suits me."

Anderson was inclined to agree. He hoped to see more of it after dinner. He inhaled the delicious smells coming from the kitchen, which made his stomach growl. "Do you need me to do anything, maybe open the wine?"

"That would be good," Holly said. "Other than that, just make yourself at home and dinner will be served shortly."

Anderson was glad that they seemed to have gotten past his error in judgment. As far as he was concerned, it was ancient history, and they hopefully had a lot of future to work on.

After opening the wine and pouring it into two goblets, Anderson sipped some while admiring photographs in the living room of Holly and two people he assumed were her parents. They had obviously both passed on their best qualities to her. Within a few minutes, Holly called him to the dining room.

"The food looks delicious," Anderson said as they sat at an oval glass-top table.

"Thanks," Holly said, beaming. Inwardly, she breathed

a sigh of relief that he liked what she had prepared. "I love cooking, but don't do it often enough."

"Yeah, I know what you mean. Between work and other activities, the art of fine cooking has had to take a backseat these days."

"Tell me about it." Holly really was glad to have Anderson in her home for the first time. She avoided any talk of him trying to mix business with their personal lives, since they had gotten past that and could now once again focus on them. She watched Anderson eating, believing that food really was the key to a man's heart. "Be sure to save room for dessert," she said playfully.

Anderson swallowed and dabbed a napkin to the corner of his mouth. "Count on it." He hoped that dessert might extend beyond cake or pie, to something that tapped into his carnal taste buds. "So tell me about your childhood."

Her eyes widened. "You really want to know?"

"Yes, I'd like to know everything about you."

She blushed and was happy to share. "I had a wonderful childhood. My parents doted over me and my brother, Stuart, and probably spoiled us too much."

"I don't know about that," Anderson said, lifting a fork with mashed potatoes. "I don't think parents can ever spoil their children too much. After all, the time they have together can be so fleeting."

Holly thought about how young Anderson had been when his mother died, depriving him of her affection during those precious formative years when perhaps he needed her most. "You're right about that." She decided not to bring up his absent father again, knowing that had been a point of contention previously.

Anderson sensed that Holly was probably thinking about his uneasiness about his father. He wanted her to feel comfortable broaching subjects with him, even if they were hard to deal with.

"I've started to look into who my father might be. I want to find out if he's still alive, and, if so, where he's living."

That surprised Holly. "That's good to know. I'm sure it's difficult and you may not get the answers you want, but at least you will have tried."

"Those are my sentiments as well." He met her eyes. "Thanks for pressing me on this."

"Sometimes I may go overboard in speaking my mind," she admitted. "But if it helps you, then it was worth it."

"Yeah, I think so."

"I hope it works out for you," Holly said, biting into a muffin.

"Me too." Anderson leaned forward. "In fact, I'd say it's working out pretty well so far."

She felt the same way.

Anderson got up and moved to a chair on her side of the table. He angled his head just right and planted a kiss on those luscious lips of hers.

Holly closed her eyes and relished the kiss, returning it with equal desire. Like before, it was a wonderful kiss that aroused her and left her wanting more and more of him.

Anderson put his hand around Holly's neck to better hold them in place for the kiss, which enveloped him from head to toe, causing flashes of light to go off in his head. He didn't want this moment to end.

The ringing of the doorbell caught them both off guard. They pulled away from the kiss.

"Expecting more company?" Anderson asked, disappointed with the timing.

"Not that I know of." Holly bit back her frustration that their kiss had been disrupted.

The bell rang again.

Anderson looked at her. "I think you'd better get that."

"Don't move," she told him. "I'll get rid of whoever it is, and we can get back to where we were."

He smiled yearningly. "I'd like that."

Holly opened the door to see her father. Since he almost never dropped by, and certainly not unannounced, her first thought was that something was wrong.

"Dad—"

"Hello," he said. "Sorry for barging in on you like this—"

"Is everything all right?" she asked.

"I'm fine," he said. "Are you?"

"Yes. Did you hear otherwise?"

"Actually, I talked to your brother and he suggested I check on you. Since I was in the neighborhood, I decided to stop by."

Holly recalled sharing some of her frustrations about

Anderson with Stuart but hadn't expected him to pass it on to their father.

"Please come in," she told her father, figuring it was as good a time as any to tell him she was seeing someone.

Anderson, curious about the visitor, had left the table and walked toward the foyer just as Holly was showing her father in.

"Didn't know you had company," Robert said as he laid eyes on Anderson.

"Dad, this is Anderson Gunn," Holly said evenly. "Anderson, my father, Robert."

"Nice to meet you, sir," Anderson said, sticking out a hand to shake his.

"You too." Robert shook his hand.

Anderson could see the clear resemblance between father and daughter. He could also see that Holly seemed slightly uncomfortable with the unplanned meeting and sought to put her at ease. "I'm guessing that you're a Houston Texans fan like me?"

"Oh yeah, big fan," Robert said.

"I've got season tickets in a choice location," Anderson said. "Maybe you can come with me to see our team kick some ass."

Robert grinned widely. "Sure, I'd like that."

"Good." Anderson smiled at Holly. "We'll set it up."

Anderson was for sure earning brownie points with Holly.

"We were just finishing up dinner," she told her father. "There's still food left, if you'd like something."

Robert shook his head. "No, I already ate. I can see you're busy, so I'll leave you two alone."

"You can stay for a few minutes," Holly said. Now that he had met Anderson, she might as well see how they got along. So far so good.

"All right," Robert said.

"Can I get you a glass of wine?" she asked.

"Yeah, okay." He sat in the living room and Anderson joined him. "So are you dating my daughter?"

"Yes, sir," Anderson said straightforwardly.

"Call me Robert."

"All right." Anderson was only too happy to have him as an ally.

Robert stretched his legs, studying him. "What do you do for a living, Anderson?"

"I'm a legal consultant."

"So you're a lawyer?" Robert asked.

Anderson nodded. "Yes. Used to practice law in the corporate world, but now I work with law firms to strengthen their positions."

"I see. And where did you and Holly meet?"

"At the airport a while back," Anderson responded.

Holly caught that last part as she came in with wine for her father and a refill for Anderson. "Hope you're not being grilled too much by my father."

He laughed. "Not at all. Just having a friendly conversation."

"That's right," Robert said, taking the glass of wine from her. "Why didn't you tell me you were involved with someone?"

She exchanged glances with Anderson. "I would've gotten around to it sooner or later," she said, sitting in a chair. "We both wanted to see how things went first."

"And I take it things are going well for you?" he asked directly.

She smiled. "Yes, we're enjoying each other's company."

"Good thing, because I don't want to miss the opportunity to sit in good seats and watch the Texans play."

Anderson chuckled. "Don't worry about that. You'll definitely get to be there to watch them beat up some other team."

Robert laughed. "One could only hope it's not the other way around."

"Not a chance," he said.

Robert finished his wine and stood. "Well, I've got another stop to make, so I'll leave you two to your date."

"I'll walk you out," Holly said. She wanted a moment alone with him to get his opinion of Anderson.

"Sure. Nice meeting you, Anderson."

"You too, Robert." He shook his hand again. "I'll be in touch regarding the game."

"You do that."

"Be right back," Holly whispered to Anderson as her father walked to the door. "Try not to miss me too much."

He grinned. "Won't be easy, but I'll do my best."

Holly stepped outside where her father was standing on the porch. "Hey," she said.

"Hey." Robert put his hand on her shoulder. "Is he the one your brother was somewhat concerned about?"

"Yes," Holly admitted. "It was no big deal really."

"If you say so."

"I do. No need to worry about me, Dad."

"I'm not," he said. "I know you're a big girl and can take care of yourself."

"I try to," she said.

"Anderson seems like a nice fellow."

"He is nice," Holly said. "We get along well."

Robert peered at her. "Is it serious?"

"Not right now. But maybe we're moving in that direction, slowly but surely."

"Slow is good. No need to rush into anything. If he's the right one for you in the long haul, you'll know it soon enough."

"I'm sure you're right," she agreed. "Well, I'd better get back inside."

He kissed her cheek. "Your mother would be pretty proud of you right now."

"You really think so?"

"I know so. And your brother, too. Now get going, and I'll see you later."

Holly's eyes crinkled at him as she waved goodbye. It was hard to adjust to the fact that he was starting to get up there in years. She wondered if Anderson thought about his father when he met hers and if it had made him wonder what it would have been like to attend a football game with his own father.

Chapter 8

Holly stepped back inside to find Anderson clearing dishes from the dining room table.

"You don't have to do that," she said.

"I don't mind," he told her. "I'm happy to help out."

Your being here has helped more than I can say, she thought, moving toward him. "Thank you."

Anderson smiled. "It was my pleasure." He put the last dish on the counter in the kitchen. "I hope I passed the father test."

Holly chuckled. "Yes, I believe you did." Indeed, she could not remember anyone she had dated previously who had gotten off to such a good start with her father, which was definitely a positive sign. "It was nice of you to offer to take him to a football game."

Anderson shrugged. "It was no big deal. I usually take clients to butter them up."

She grinned. "Ah, so you want to butter my dad up, do you?"

He chuckled warmly. "Well, it never hurts to get the old man on my side."

"Very true," Holly said. "And I'd say it's working."

"Good." Anderson took her in his arms. "I seem to recall that we were enjoying a rather nice kiss before we were interrupted."

"Hmm…I seem to recall the same thing," she said.

"What are we going to do about that?"

She batted her eyes coquettishly. "What would you *like* to do about it?"

Anderson looked into her eyes squarely, full of desire for her. "Just this—"

He tilted his head slightly and began to kiss her. She returned the kiss in full and Anderson quickly gave her mouth his undivided attention, loving every moment of it.

Holly felt light on her feet, as the powerful kiss left her helpless to this man and the sexual energy passing between them like bolts of lightning.

By the time she unlocked their mouths, Holly felt totally overwhelmed by Anderson. "Maybe we should postpone the peach cobbler," she said on a quick breath.

His eyes pinned on her—he wanted her more than ever.

"Yes, maybe we should."

Holly took him by the hand and led him silently

to her bedroom. She began to remove her clothes and watched with great anticipation as he did the same. He looked sexy from his head to his bare feet.

Anderson took only a sweeping glance of the room, noting the elegant cherrywood furniture set, before returning his focus to the beautiful woman before him. She was even more beautiful as the clothing vanished from her body and he got to take in her naked perfection, beginning with her small, nicely rounded breasts and a shapely body that was taut in all the right places.

Grabbing a condom from his pants pocket, Anderson quickly slipped it onto his erection. He was barely able to contain himself, knowing the moist warmth of her body was sure to captivate him to no end.

He scooped her up in his arms and carried her to the sleigh bed. He placed her on top of the bedspread, then joined her. He brought his mouth to hers for a delicious kiss. When he slid between her legs and entered her, she was wet and very ready for him.

Holly welcomed the feel of Anderson inside her, coaxing him deeper within as she held on to his firm buttocks. She arched her back, bringing her breasts up to his chest, then sought out his lips again. They made love as if they were already completely familiar with one another's body.

As her orgasm began, Holly gasped, feeling the surge spread joyously throughout her entire body. She trembled and clung to her lover while he too quavered with the release of his orgasm.

Anderson let out a deep breath, stifling the urge to moan, as the powerful sensations of satisfaction overcame him. He thrust harder into Holly, her cries urging him on, kissing her face, neck, ears and mouth lustfully and riding the waves of passion and pleasure.

They both enjoyed every second of sexual appeasement till they were spent and content in the afterglow.

Anderson gave Holly one final succulent kiss before rolling off her and onto the bed. "You were amazing," he said.

"Look who's talking," Holly responded unabashedly. "I think we were both pretty amazing."

"I couldn't agree more." Anderson kissed her shoulder. "Some things in life are well worth the wait. This was certainly one of them."

"So you were waiting for this?" she asked playfully.

He grinned. "Weren't you?"

"Well, I wasn't exactly counting down the seconds, but the thought did cross my mind as to how nice it would be to make love to you."

It pleased Anderson to know that she obviously wanted him as badly as he wanted her. "Fortunately, we can keep making love to each other."

"Are we already planning the next time?" Holly asked, feeling remarkably comfortable talking to him about sex, even as they lay there naked.

"Yeah, and the next ten times," he said with a wink.

Making love to Anderson only made Holly's desire to have him that much stronger. But, at the same time, she didn't want them to get too ahead of themselves.

"For now, let's just enjoy the moment," she said.

"That's exactly what I'm doing," Anderson said with a kiss.

The next week, Anderson was in his office doing his usual videoconferencing with clients and giving them advice. He found it hard to focus when Holly always seemed to be at the forefront of his mind. She had left an indelible impression on him mentally, physically and sexually, and he was determined to build upon what they had begun to establish.

When his assistant buzzed and told him that John Lacey was there to see him, Anderson asked her to wait five minutes before sending him in. It gave him time to wrap up things with the videoconference and set up the next meeting.

He stood up, straightening his tie and buttoning the jacket of his gray suit coat. He watched as the private investigator he had hired to search for his long-lost father entered the office. Anderson hadn't expected to hear from him so soon.

"Mr. Gunn, I hope I didn't catch you at a bad time," John Lacey said.

"Not at all," Anderson told him. He shook the hand of the fortysomething man with gray hair and glasses.

"I've got some information for you."

Anderson tensed as he considered the possibility that his father was dead. Or, just as unsettling in some ways, that he was alive and well and living in Houston.

"Why don't we sit down," he told the detective as

he pointed at some comfortable chairs surrounding a round table.

John sat and put his briefcase on the table. "As you know, I didn't have very much information to go on, trying to locate your father. But I did have the name listed on your birth certificate as the father—Chester Gunn." He opened the briefcase and took out a sheet of paper, handing it to Anderson.

"What's this?" he asked before studying it.

"It's a list of all the Chester Gunns I've come up with so far that fit the age range your father would likely be. As you can see, it is not exactly a common name, but not so unique either."

Anderson could see that there were around twelve people named Chester Gunn. Only two lived in Texas, with the rest scattered across the country. He looked at the detective. "You think my father is one of these men?"

"It's possible," John said. "It's also possible that he's dead or using another name now. I'd like to contact all of these men and either eliminate them from the list or further pursue leads, as well as check out any others who come up that may give you the answers you need."

"Do whatever is necessary," Anderson said. He took out his checkbook and made out a check for a generous amount, then handed it to him. "Will that cover your expenses?"

John nodded. "Yes, I believe it will. As soon as I have anything else pertinent, I'll let you know."

"Sounds good." Anderson stood. "You have my cell phone number."

"I'll be in touch," John said after getting up. The two shook hands again.

"Have a good day," Anderson said. He saw him out before going back in the office and calling Holly.

"Hello, handsome," she answered in a bubbly voice.

"Hello, gorgeous," he responded. "Doing anything special for lunch?"

"No, nothing special. Why?"

"I'd like to take you somewhere for a great lunch and to share some news."

"I'm game, and I'm intrigued," Holly said.

"Good. I'll pick you up in half an hour, if that's not too soon," Anderson said.

"It isn't. I'll see you then."

Anderson had mixed feelings about his father and what he would say to him if they were to meet face-to-face. He had no illusion that they would have the type of warm and loving relationship Holly had with her father. But it didn't mean he was above being cordial to the man, even though he had never hung around long enough to do right by him or his mother.

Anderson felt he owed Holly for at least getting him to think outside his self-imposed box. She was doing things to him that made Anderson wonder where she had been all his life. He wondered if it would have changed some of his past mistakes had she been the one he'd fallen in love with once upon a time.

* * *

Holly rode with Anderson, curious as to where they would have lunch. He was being mysterious about it, leaving her curiosity all the more piqued. And what else was on his mind, she wondered. It felt good to be dating someone who seemed to be making the right moves in his life. She could only wonder if it would last.

"Here we are," Anderson said, interrupting her thoughts as he pulled into the parking lot of the soup kitchen.

Holly cocked a brow. "This is where we're having lunch?"

He smiled, hoping it wouldn't be too much of a turn-off for her. "The food is surprisingly good," he said. "Besides, it seemed like a good way for you to meet Esther Wright. She runs the place."

"Uh, all right." Holly was a little thrown off by having lunch at a soup kitchen usually reserved for the homeless. But she wasn't so snooty that she'd refuse to eat there. On the contrary, she admired that Anderson—whom she imagined probably often ate at five-star restaurants—was so down-to-earth that he was willing to eat at a soup kitchen and give of his time there.

Anderson appreciated that Holly was willing to keep an open mind. It was important to know that she wasn't the type of person who thought they were better than everyone else was.

They went inside and found Esther. "Well, hello there," she said with a bright smile.

"Hi, Miss Wright," Anderson said.

"And who do we have with you today?"

"This is Holly."

Esther's eyes crinkled. "You must be the wonderful lady Anderson told me about. Welcome to the soup kitchen." She gave her a hug.

"I'm happy to be here," Holly said, peeking at Anderson, who had obviously become close to the older woman.

"Are you here to work?" Esther asked hopefully.

"Actually, we're here for a square meal first," Anderson surprised her by saying. "Then we'll pitch in with serving."

"Sounds fine to me. You're always welcome here."

"Thanks." Anderson kissed her cheek. "Now we're ready to chow down."

"Then chow down you will," Esther said.

They stood in the serving line and received a helping of roast beef and gravy, rice, corn and carrot cake.

Anderson led Holly to a table, where they both sat.

"You're full of surprises," she told him.

"Good or bad?" he wondered, slicing the roast beef.

"Definitely good." She dug her spoon into the corn and ate some. "I can't say I've ever eaten in a soup kitchen before, but the food is tasty."

He smiled. "Glad you like it. The cooks take their work seriously, and they really try to treat those less fortunate with a meal fit for a king. Or queen."

Holly laughed. "So I'm a queen, huh?"

"You are to me," he said earnestly.

"Why, thank you." She blushed. "I think you've got the royalty thing going on, too."

Anderson chuckled. "I'll settle for Prince Charming."

"You certainly fit the bill," she had to admit.

He grinned, loving how naturally their conversation flowed. There was clearly something going on here that he didn't want to see end anytime soon.

Anderson ate some rice and met Holly's eyes. "I may have a lead on my father."

"Oh." She held his gaze with interest. "What?"

He told her what the detective had discovered thus far. "Whether any of these men turns out to be the real deal remains to be seen, but at least it's something to go on." He still hadn't decided if he was happy about that, given the fact that he didn't know what his father would be like.

"I'm glad that the detective seems to be making progress," Holly said. "Hopefully this will lead to something positive." She was fully aware that his father, if still alive, could reject him. Or, worse, not even acknowledge him. But she believed in that old adage: nothing ventured, nothing gained.

"I hope that, too," Anderson said. For now, he was more than content to live with the knowledge that she was the one who had opened his eyes to this search.

Holly continued to eat the food, which really was delicious, before she turned her thoughts to an event coming up soon.

"Next Wednesday is the broadcast journalist banquet

downtown," she informed Anderson. "Would you like to be my date?"

He pretended to be mentally checking his schedule before bursting into a pleased smile. "Absolutely! Count me in."

"Great." She grinned, certain she would easily have the most handsome man on her arm.

After they finished eating, Anderson and Holly took a spot in the serving line, dishing out food.

Anderson found Holly to be a natural with her friendly chatter. She made each person feel that he or she was being given her undivided attention—something he could certainly relate to. She was certainly giving him the kind of personal attention that rocked his world and made him want to give back just as much in return.

Chapter 9

The broadcast journalist banquet was held in the ballroom of a luxury hotel. Holly entered on Anderson's arm. She was wearing a dark teal pleated evening gown and sable pumps. Her hair was up and a pearl necklace matched her earrings. She remembered his comment about her being a queen, and she really felt the part this evening as his date.

She looked up at him—he was resplendent in a black tux. "Welcome to my world," she told him.

Anderson grinned, feeling just a bit out of his league, but happy nonetheless to be in Holly's company. "It should be fun," he said.

"At the very least, it will be interesting," Holly promised, knowing that these functions were often unpredictable.

They sat with Blythe and her co-anchor, Allan Kennedy. The two seemed to be more than a little cozy and Holly wondered if they were actually dating.

"Nice to see you again, Anderson," Blythe said.

"You too." He smiled.

"Maybe you can be Holly's good luck charm for winning an award, just as I'm hoping Allan will be mine."

Anderson knew that Holly had been nominated for Outstanding Broadcast Journalist in Houston. Though she had downplayed her chances of winning, he didn't see why she should not win, since she was a damned good anchorwoman.

"I'm happy to be her good luck charm," he said, gazing at Holly. "Whatever it takes."

Holly blushed. This was the second time she'd been nominated for an award. After being disappointed when she didn't win the last time, she refused to get her hopes up too high only to have them come crashing down. "We're all winners at this table, no matter what happens," she said diplomatically.

"My sentiments precisely," Allan said, raising his wineglass so they could all toast to that.

A few minutes later, Holly and Blythe went to the powder room.

"You two really make a lovely couple," Blythe said, applying lip gloss.

"We do, don't we?" Holly said. "But then, so do you and Allan. Or am I mistaken about the hard-to-miss vibes passing between you two?"

Blythe smiled. "No, you're not mistaken. We've recently started seeing each other. I know what you're thinking, that there's a few years' age difference between us. But I've always been attracted to older men. This one just happens to be my colleague, and he's newly single like me, and great to look at and sleep with."

Holly grinned. "Well, you go, girl," she declared. "I wish you and Allan nothing but the best."

"Same for you and Anderson," Blythe said. "We deserve to be happy with the men in our lives."

"Yes, we do." Holly put a touch of blush on her cheeks. "So why not create our own happiness?"

"Exactly. Speaking of happy times, Sharon Pickford, who does the evening news with Scott Turner, is going on maternity leave next month. I've been asked to take her place while she's off, and there's a good chance it will be permanent."

"Oh, that's wonderful news," Holly said, giving her a hug. "It's what you've wanted."

"It is. Everything suddenly seems to be falling into place."

"Ditto."

They got back to the table just in time to hear the nominees' names being read. Holly, who had a prepared speech in case she won, felt her heart pounding. She braced herself for the possibility that the award could just as easily go to one of the other talented people in the running. And how would she come across to Anderson if she lost? Would he think any less of her talents as a journalist?

As the winner was being announced, Holly felt Anderson reach out and take her hand. He smiled at her and she acknowledged with a smile of her own before facing the stage and holding her breath for what seemed like an eternity.

"And the winner of the city's Outstanding Broadcast Journalist award is…Holly Kendall!"

Holly was overcome with joy. As she stood, trying to wrap her mind around the results, Anderson gave her a soulful congratulatory kiss.

"I'm so happy for you," he whispered. "You deserve this."

"Thank you," she told him, flashing a toothy smile.

Holly graciously accepted the award, making sure to acknowledge her fellow nominees, who were surely as disappointed as she would have been. She had bragging rights for the next year, and along with it, the responsibility of measuring up to the achievement.

Anderson and Holly went back to his place to continue the celebration. They wasted little time stripping off their clothes and getting into bed. Each wanted the other more and more with every touch, caress and kiss, but they took their time in a slow and sensual seduction.

Holly placed the latex over Anderson's erection then climbed on him, aching for the fulfillment that only he could give her. She lowered herself onto his hard body and felt him enter her, sending streaks of fire throughout her body as she moved up and down the incredible length of him. He played with her breasts and nipples, further exciting her, before pulling her body down to his, where their mouths joined in mutual harmony.

They made love with utter abandon as their hot bodies glistened from the frenetic movement. Holly could not remember a time when she felt so alive and in tune with another human being. She seemed to be floating on air, but knew that Anderson would be there to catch her should she fall from his heavenly embrace.

Anderson easily turned them over, thrusting himself into Holly's warm and moist core, and feeling overjoyed as she met him halfway with each thrust. He inhaled her intoxicating scent and ran his fingers through the silky strands of her hair while they kissed as though there were no tomorrow.

He fought hard to hold back from reaching the peak of satisfaction, so that they could climax together. Clutching Holly's buttocks, Anderson moved even deeper inside her, wanting to scream with pleasure as her contractions grew stronger around him as the pace of their lovemaking quickened.

Holly clawed at Anderson's back and bit his shoulder as her orgasm came with a jolt, sending her into a state of ecstasy. She cried out with joy, continuing to propel her body at him, wanting his pleasure to be just as powerful.

Within moments, Anderson's release came and he held on tightly to her while devouring her juicy lips and allowing the exquisite sensations to take effect.

Both rode the wave of pleasure for all it was worth

before settling down and allowing their perspiring bodies and beating hearts to return to normal.

"What a way to cap off a wonderful evening," Holly said after a deep breath.

"You're telling me," Anderson said huskily, untangling their limbs and climbing off her. "Maybe you need to win some awards more often."

She giggled. "I think what just happened had less to do with the award and more with the two people in bed right now."

"Sounds about right." He kissed one of her breasts. "Guess we just can't get enough of each other."

"Guess we can't." Holly was starting to realize that she had a thing for him that she had never had for anyone before. It scared her, since it left her vulnerable to being hurt. But she also embraced having such a fulfilling physical and emotional relationship after being alone for so long.

Anderson gently ran his hand across the side of her face. He found it hard to resist touching her at every opportunity. "Some things are just meant to be."

Holly propped up on an elbow. "And you think we're one of those things?"

"Don't you?"

"I've never really believed in fate, per se," she said honestly. "I think that people make their own connections and their own destiny."

"I can't argue with that," he said. "But if those connections are lasting, then isn't it all the same difference?"

"I suppose so." Holly put her hand on his muscular chest, sending a fresh wave of desire through her.

"As long as it's working, there is no greater satisfaction than being with a person who seems so right for you."

"We do seem pretty right for each other," she murmured, running her foot up his leg.

Anderson reacted to the stimulation of her toes on his body. "Are we looking to go another round?"

"Are you up for it?" she challenged, even though his arousal spoke for itself.

"Always," he said.

Over the next half hour they enjoyed each other's bodies, covering every angle and inventing new ones while their bodies absorbed the intense sensations.

When it was over, Anderson held Holly in his arms.

"I have to go to San Francisco for business next week," he said.

"For how long?" she asked, hating the thought of being without him for any length of time.

"Shouldn't be more than a couple of days."

"I suppose I'll just have to try and get along without you," she said, half teasing.

"I have a better idea," Anderson said. "Why don't you come with me?" He was finding it more and more difficult to be apart from her.

"Are you serious?"

"Of course," he said. "My business won't take up too much of my time. Why not make it a little romantic getaway? There's no place more romantic than the City by the Bay."

"Hmm…"

"Don't worry," he said, "if there's any turbulence, I'll be there to protect you."

She chuckled. "Promise?"

He grinned. "Yes, you'll be safe with me."

Holly didn't doubt that for one minute. "I'd love to go to San Francisco with you."

"Wonderful." Anderson beamed. "Now, how about if we seal that with a kiss?"

"You'll get no argument from me," she said.

He kissed her heartily and they made love again before sleeping through the night in each other's arms.

Chapter 10

On the day before they were to fly to San Francisco, Anderson accompanied Holly to two local elementary schools where they read classics to the children. Anderson enjoyed chipping in and seemed to have won over the students pretty quickly. He liked it even better, though, when he listened to Holly read as if she were in a Broadway play. She was clearly in the zone and giving her audience something they could really learn from.

Anderson enjoyed it so much that he had no doubt that he would become a regular participant in the literary program.

That afternoon, they had lunch in the Union Building cafeteria on the University of Houston campus. It brought back memories for both of them of their days as students.

"I'll just bet you were quite a player in those days," joked Holly. She was about to dig in to a corned beef sandwich.

"Not really," he said, sipping soda through a straw. "I was too busy trying to keep my grades up."

"So you were a brainiac?"

He laughed. "I wouldn't go quite that far." He lifted a fry and dipped it into ketchup. "I had my share of fun, but never lost sight of my true goals in life."

"Neither did I," Holly said. "Too bad our lives didn't intersect then. Who knows what trouble we may have gotten ourselves into?"

Anderson chuckled. "Probably lots of trouble." He leaned forward. "I'd say we're doing a good job of making up for it now."

Holly colored. "We are, aren't we?" She loved that they could be so free in sharing their feelings, something she hadn't experienced previously in dating. She wondered if that was a good indicator for the future.

"You'll get no complaints whatsoever from my end," he told her.

"Or mine," she said.

Anderson grabbed a fry and held it up to Holly's mouth. She bit off a piece.

"Satisfied?" she teased.

"Perfectly." He laughed while he watched her chew it and then sexily lick off some ketchup from the corner of her mouth. There was no doubt in his mind that they were headed for even bigger and better things in their relationship.

After lunch, Anderson paid a courtesy call to the law school, where he had become somewhat of a role model. He proudly introduced Holly to a couple of his old professors. She seemed excited to meet them, and they recognized her as an anchorwoman and local celebrity.

Finally Anderson took Holly to meet his close friend Lester Powell, who taught law at the school part-time.

"Very nice to finally meet you," Lester told Holly in his office.

"You too," she said, shaking his hand.

"This dude hasn't been able to stop talking about you," Lester claimed.

Holly smiled, a little embarrassed. "I'll have to get on him about that," she said lightly.

"What can I say," Anderson said with a grin. "Some things—or people—are worth talking about."

"Amen to that," Lester said, giving him a high five.

"Oh, stop it, you two," Holly said.

Lester looked at her. "I hear this is your alma mater, too."

"You heard right," she told him proudly.

"Cool. And you obviously made good use of your education. I've seen you on the news. You really know how to get to the heart of the story."

"It's called practice makes perfect," she told him.

"Well, whatever it is, it works." He tapped Anderson on the shoulder. "Certainly does for this man here."

Holly's eyes twinkled. "He works for me, too."

Anderson put his arm around her and kissed her cheek. "Guess that's why we get along so well." He could tell that she'd already left a favorable impression on Lester, which he would surely confirm later. But even so, Anderson didn't need to be told that they made a perfect couple.

Anderson and Holly arrived in San Francisco after a remarkably smooth flight. In fact, Holly had even fallen asleep on Anderson's shoulder and woken up just before they landed with his arm around her affectionately. She couldn't help but feel that they were made for each other.

They checked in to their hotel suite overlooking downtown San Francisco, and Anderson opened a bottle of champagne that was awaiting them, courtesy of the hotel. He poured it in two flutes, handing one to Holly.

"Welcome to the City by the Bay," he said, smiling at her.

"I'm happy to be here with you," she said as she took a sip of the champagne.

"I promise that we'll make the most of this romantic escape."

Holly grinned. "I'm counting on it."

With that, they kissed, keeping their mouths locked long enough for Holly to feel the buildup of desire within her that was threatening to explode. But she knew that Anderson was set to meet with clients shortly, so she suppressed her need for him and pulled away.

Using her pinkie to wipe lip gloss from his mouth, she said, "We can get back to that when you return."

Anderson frowned, wishing to hell he could simply

postpone the business aspects of his trip and spend all the time with Holly, so they could continue to explore the passions they brought out in each other. But he appreciated that she had no problem with him doing a little work, and he knew they would make up for it later.

He smiled. "I won't be too long," he promised.

"Better not," she teased. "I'm sure I can find ways to keep myself busy while you're out. I love to shop and San Francisco has some of the finest stores in the world. Or so I've heard. Might as well take full advantage of them."

"I couldn't agree more." Anderson hoped that later they might even do a little shopping together, along with seeing the sights and sounds of the city. Most importantly, though, he wanted to spend some quality romantic time with Holly away from home.

An hour later, Holly was already missing Anderson, but she was determined not to crowd him. *I'll see him when I do,* she thought. *In the meantime, I plan to make the most of this experience.*

Holly was back in the room sipping cappuccino and relaxing when her cell phone rang. She saw that it was Madison calling. Holly had left her a voice mail earlier.

"I am so envious," Madison said. "I love San Francisco."

"It is nice here." Holly felt a little guilty being on this trip with a man while Madison was still trying to deal with a breakup. But she would not let that take away from her romantic visit to the city, knowing that her own happiness in a relationship was just as important.

"I've been there a couple of times for work. They have one of the largest annual book fairs in the world every February."

"I didn't realize that," Holly said.

"Pumps a lot of money into the local economy with people coming from all over," Madison said.

"I'm sure." Holly would love to be there someday for the book fair and share her love of books with Anderson.

"So what are you two planning while there?" Madison wondered.

"I think we'll pretty much play it by ear," Holly told her, though there were a few things they had already agreed upon. "I'm sure we'll be spending a lot of time in our hotel suite," she giggled.

"That'll be fun." Madison paused. "Seriously, I want you to do all the things couples who are really into each other do."

"What about you?" Holly asked. "Any prospects on the horizon?"

"None that I know of. But hey, anything can happen, right?"

"Absolutely." Holly considered that her friend Blythe had found someone, as had she. That left only Madison to make it complete among her girlfriends.

"Well, I'd better let you get back to having fun in San Francisco. I'll see you when you get back," Madison said.

"I'll call you," Holly promised, "and we'll set up something."

* * *

Holly went shopping in the Union Square District, picking up some professional and casual clothing. She also decided it might be a nice time to buy some sexy lingerie. Even though Anderson seemed to prefer her naked when they were in bed, leaving a little to the imagination from time to time was never a bad idea.

By the time she returned to the hotel, Anderson was waiting in the room. "There's my darling," he said.

She smiled, enjoying hearing this term of endearment for the first time. "Missed me, did you?"

"What's not to miss?" He kissed her.

She licked her lips, tasting his. "How was your meeting?"

"Boring as hell, to tell you the truth. Especially when compared to being with you," Anderson said.

"Good thing you didn't come all this way just for that," she said teasingly.

"That's for sure." He glanced at her bags. "Looks like someone made the local shopkeepers happy."

"I hope I make you happy, too," she said sweetly.

"Always," he insisted, grinning.

"I have something that might make you just a little happier…" Holly showed him the rose-colored satin chemise she had bought. She posed, holding the lingerie in front of her. "You like?"

Anderson was turned on. "Oh yeah, I like!"

"In that case, I'll wear it tonight and you can choose whether you want to take it off or not."

"Tough decision," he said, putting his hands on her waist and pulling her to him. "Luckily I can't lose either way."

Holly's eyes lit with desire. "Neither can I."

They went out to dinner at a fancy restaurant in the Mission District, took in a play and made love for practically the whole night through, exploring each other in the most passionate and pleasurable of ways. It gave Holly another reason to feel grateful that she had found such a wonderful man to spend time with.

The following day, Anderson met with clients in the morning, but then cut it short to spend the rest of the day with Holly so they could take in the city. They walked hand in hand on the Golden Gate Bridge, toured Fisherman's Wharf, rode a cable car, took pictures of the winding or "crooked" stretch of Lombard Street and did some shopping on Fillmore Street. Later they dined on prime rib and mashed sweet potatoes at their hotel and went dancing afterward.

By the time Holly and Anderson got back to their room, they were exhausted but still up for making love. Holly could barely contain her desire for Anderson as she stripped him of his clothes.

In bed they held nothing back, engaging each other with every deep kiss, fervent touch and gentle caress. When Anderson entered her, Holly gasped sharply, drawing him in deeper and arching her back as she experienced the immense pleasure. She constricted around him, wanting him to achieve total fulfillment from their union.

Anderson reacted as he moved forward between Holly's splayed legs, their mouths locked in harmony and bodies pressed together. He could not seem to get enough of his lover, her scent, touch and everything about her. He could imagine them making love till they were old and gray, were they so fortunate to make such a committed life together.

It was Holly who came first, levitating and crying out as the orgasm wrapped itself around her and sent glorious spasms of pleasure throughout her body. She sucked on Anderson's lower lip, and then slipped her tongue inside his mouth, tasting the wine he'd had earlier. She ran her hands across his head, and then held on to it while soaking in the passions of their sex.

His climax came shortly thereafter, causing Anderson's body to quiver wildly and his hot breath to brush over her cheeks. Holly wrapped her legs and arms around his back, meeting his powerful thrusts with equal abandon as she had another orgasm at the same time he reached the peak of sexual satisfaction.

They ended with a powerful kiss. As they lay spent, side by side, Anderson felt closer to Holly in that moment than he had to anyone in his life. Which made it easier to say what he knew was true. He faced her; she was beautiful as ever in the afterglow of sex.

"I'm falling in love with you," he murmured.

"Oh really?"

Anderson touched her shoulder. "Yes, really."

Holly let the words sink in for a moment. "Are you sure it's your heart speaking and not something below the waist?"

"Quite sure," he said. "You've come to mean that much to me." Now he hoped to hear the same magical words from her. Would he?

Holly had waited a long time to hear such sweet words from a man. How could she not share the same sentiments when Anderson did things to her mind and body that no other man had?

"I'm falling in love with you, too," she admitted.

"Really?" Anderson asked, wanting to hear the words again.

"Yes, I'm falling in love with you, Anderson." Holly laughed and kissed his mouth joyously.

He laughed back and kissed her. "What a perfect way to end our stay in San Francisco."

"I agree," Holly said.

They made love again and Anderson saw nothing but blue skies over the horizon for them. He felt they were laying the foundation for what promised to be a passionate relationship that, in his mind, was for keeps.

Chapter 11

A week later, Holly and Anderson were relaxing at her place, watching television and eating popcorn. To Holly, it felt comfortable, as if they had been together forever.

She fed Anderson some popcorn, chuckling as he gobbled it down. "You know, you're cute with this popcorn," she teased.

"I'll be as cute as you like," he said, kissing her. "As long as you stay as beautiful as you are."

"I'll do my best."

The doorbell rang.

"Looks like you've got company," Anderson said, not especially looking forward to sharing their alone time. But he didn't want to take up all of her time away from the job and knew he had to give her the space she needed.

"I think it might be my girlfriend," Holly said, standing. "She told me she might drop by to meet you."

He grinned. "Ah, so you want to show me off to your friends, huh?"

"Maybe just a little," she admitted. "Can I help it if I want everyone to know how fortunate I am to have you?"

Anderson smiled and grabbed her hand before she could leave. "That works both ways you know. I'm looking forward to introducing you to more of my friends," he assured her.

"You're so sweet." Holly leaned over the couch and kissed him before reluctantly heading for the door. With their attraction to each other and sexual chemistry, it was a wonder they managed to spend any time apart.

Holly opened the door to find Madison standing there. "Hey," she said.

"Hey," Madison responded. "Is he here?"

"Sure is—just waiting for your appraisal," Holly kidded. "Promise me you'll be nice."

"I'm always nice, girl. You know that."

Holly chuckled. "In that case, come on in…"

Madison stepped inside. Her eyes immediately turned to the living room, where she observed Anderson sitting on the couch. Her mouth dropped. "You!"

Holly met Anderson's eyes, clueless as to what her friend meant.

Anderson thought the voice sounded familiar but wasn't quite able to place it. It wasn't until he saw Madison—her eyes like razor slits—that he realized Holly's friend was none other than the woman he had been engaged to two years ago.

"What the hell is he doing here?" Madison demanded.

"You two know each other?" Holly asked.

"You're damned right we do," she said sharply. "Will you tell her, or should I?"

Anderson gulped, immediately getting to his feet. This situation admittedly gave him quite a start, as Madison was the last person he had expected to show up. After all, they had not had any contact since the day he broke off the engagement. He hadn't been sure what he could have said to her at the time to smooth things over. Similar to how he was feeling at the moment.

"Yeah, we know each other," he said with a long sigh. "We were once engaged—"

Holly's eyes grew wide. "What?" she asked. She was certain she had misunderstood him.

Anderson ran a hand across his mouth, glancing at Madison then back to Holly. "Madison and I were involved two years ago."

It was all beginning to sink in to Holly. "You're the one who called off the wedding?"

As much as he wanted to deny it, Anderson knew he couldn't. Particularly not with Madison glaring at him as if she wanted to take him down. "Yes, I did, but—"

"But nothing!" Madison said angrily. "You were a bastard then, and you're a bastard now."

"Let me try and explain," he said.

"You're two years and too many tears late for that."

Madison's nostrils flared. "I don't want to hear anything you have to say." She turned to Holly. "If I were you, I'd kick him to the curb as fast as you can before he dumps you like he did me."

Holly was at a loss for words as she looked at both of them. "I had no idea Anderson was the man who called off your engagement," she told Madison.

"Well, now you know." Madison shot Anderson a cold look before turning to Holly. "I'm out of here."

"Wait…" Holly called out, but Madison ignored her and stormed out the door. Facing Anderson, Holly furrowed her brow. "Don't just stand there—go after her," she said.

Anderson sucked in a deep breath. He had thought about doing that very thing, but didn't see the point. "She doesn't want to hear anything I have to say."

"You don't know that," Holly said.

"Yes, I do. No need to go back down memory lane for something I can't change. Let it go."

"I wish I could, but Madison's my friend and she's hurting now because of you." Holly grabbed her purse. "I have to find her. If you want to leave, that's fine."

"I don't want to go anywhere," he told her. "I just want us to keep things as they are."

"Not sure we can." *If it were only that simple,* she thought.

Holly left in search of Madison. How had she not put two and two together? Was there any chance she could keep one without losing the other when this was over? Would she even want to stay with Anderson, who obviously had a problem with commitment—something she didn't need in a man with whom she had fallen in love.

Anderson flopped back down on the couch and grabbed his bottle of beer off the coffee table, taking a swig.

Damn, he thought, trying to wrap his mind around the fact that Madison Wagner was suddenly back in his life. Deep down inside he had known that somehow his past would come back to haunt him. Now it had actually happened.

How could he try to explain to Holly what had gone down between him and Madison, while at the same time trying to distance himself from it? He was sure Madison would bad-mouth him to the woman he loved and who had professed to love him. Would that all change now?

Anderson drank more beer. The TV was still on, as was the movie they had been watching. What were the odds that Holly and Madison would be friends in a city the size of Houston? He hadn't seen that coming. For all he knew, Madison had moved elsewhere, gotten a fresh start and met a new man. But whether there was a new man in her life, she was obviously still in town.

And still pissed as hell at him for ending their relationship prematurely. Never mind the fact that prolonging their inevitable breakup would have only made things more difficult down the line. But he was sure she didn't see it that way.

He could only hope that Holly was able to reason with her and let bygones be bygones.

Or had he played his cards all wrong and would now pay the price?

Holly found Madison sitting in her car, fuming. *Can't say I'd feel any different if I were in her shoes and had just seen the man who broke my heart,* she thought.

She opened the passenger door and got in. "There was no way I could have known that Anderson was your ex," she said. "He never told me he was once engaged."

"Why doesn't that surprise me?" Madison rolled her eyes. "He's a player and he's been playing you just like he played me—for an idiot!"

Holly was inclined to agree with her, but still wanted to give Anderson the benefit of the doubt that what they had was real. Or did he only see them as a romance-for-the-moment type of thing, in spite of his smooth words and passionate actions to the contrary?

"Let's talk about this," Holly said. "There's a coffee shop right around the corner."

Madison wiped away a tear that had stained her cheek. "Whatever."

Holly took that as a yes and got out of the car. She watched as Madison did the same, and wondered how they would get through this, if at all.

Minutes later, they were seated at a window table.

Holly wasn't sure where to start. Or, for that matter, what this unexpected turn of events meant for the future. She was still trying to get used to the idea of Madison and Anderson once being romantically involved.

"I can't imagine what you were thinking when you walked into my house and saw him," Holly said awkwardly. *What would I have thought?*

"You don't want to know," Madison said, stone-faced. "I honestly never thought I'd ever lay eyes on Anderson again."

"Where did you two meet?" Holly asked.

"At a club in town," Madison said, sipping coffee. "It was like instant sparks that quickly turned into a wildfire—especially in bed."

A flash of jealousy passed over Holly as she thought about the two of them having sex. She couldn't help herself, given her recent sexual relationship with Anderson. Could he have ever been thinking about Madison when they were in bed together?

Holly gazed at her friend across the table. "And how long were you two together when he asked you to marry him?"

"Five months," Madison said. "At first I was like, *but we haven't known each other long enough*. But he insisted that we did and that he loved me and wanted me to be his wife. So I said yes."

"And then what?" Holly asked, feeling as if she needed to hear all the details.

"Then we made plans to get married. I picked out my dress, had the bridesmaids, the church, the reception— the whole thing was planned and set to go." Madison paused and sucked in a deep breath. "Then out of nowhere, just two weeks before I was to become his wife, Anderson called and told me it was off. No real explanation. No apology. No nothing! I was left to try and explain the unexplainable to everyone."

Holly could hardly believe that the man who had become her boyfriend would lead another woman along like that. It was almost like a real-life Dr. Jekyll and Mr. Hyde. How could he be so cruel?

Madison's eyes narrowed. "Now it's like my worst nightmare and humiliation has suddenly rematerialized, posing as your man."

"I'm so sorry about this," Holly said. She wasn't sure if she meant she was sorry about what had happened between Madison and Anderson, or the fact that she was now dating him, or both.

"Me too. But that won't make the pain go away. Or lessen the impact of seeing him with you now."

Holly sipped her drink thoughtfully. "I know how weird that seems."

"I don't think you do," Madison said. "How would you feel if one of your girlfriends was sleeping with the enemy?"

"That's not fair," she insisted. "Had I known that you and Anderson had a history when I met him, I would never have let it go any further."

"It never occurred to me that I needed to give every detail about Anderson to keep someone I called a friend away from him. And evidently he thought it best to keep his dirty little secret to himself."

Holly sighed, feeling as if she had been placed in the

middle of a war that was still going on. It was clear that she would not be able to resolve it all by herself with just a talk at a coffee shop. Not without Anderson there to give his side of the story.

Holly looked Madison in the eyes. "I don't want what happened between you and Anderson to affect our friendship."

Madison shot her a cold stare. "Well, I guess that will be up to you."

Holly got the message loud and clear. She would have to choose one or the other. And now that she saw Anderson from a whole new perspective, it didn't appear as though her choice would be too difficult.

Chapter 12

Holly wasn't sure if Anderson would still be at her house when she returned. But there he was, sprawled out on the couch, staring into space as if he had nothing better to do.

"You're still here?" she asked.

"Yeah, I wasn't going anywhere," he said glumly, looking up at Holly. "Did you talk to her?"

"Yes, and she had a lot to say." Holly crossed her arms. She was tempted to sit beside him, but decided to remain standing.

Anderson had no illusions about the ugly picture Madison had undoubtedly painted of him. All he could do now was try to defend himself and hope it was enough. "I'm sorry this went down the way it did."

"I'm not really interested in your apologies," Holly

said, glaring at him. "Why didn't you tell me you were once engaged?"

He rubbed his chin. "I told you there was someone in my past and that I made some mistakes then."

"That's not a good enough answer."

He sighed. "Because it was over and done with," he said flatly. "And it wasn't exactly the type of thing you share with someone you're romantically involved with."

"I had a right to know before things got too serious between us."

"It had nothing to do with us."

"But it had everything to do with Madison. Why on earth would you pull a stunt like that?"

"It wasn't a stunt," he said. "I just decided I wasn't ready for marriage at that time and did what I needed to do."

Holly locked eyes with him. "Why lead her on if you had no intention of marrying her?"

"I had every intention of marrying her," Anderson said. "But then I had second thoughts."

"You mean you got cold feet?"

"Something like that." He stood up. "It wasn't as simple as that—"

"Nothing ever is." She purposely kept some distance between them. If he thought for one moment that he could sweet-talk her, he was wrong. "That doesn't excuse your behavior. What type of man calls his fiancée on the phone to call off a wedding? That was really classy."

"I admit it's not one of my proudest moments. But

at the time, I didn't know how else to tell her without making things even worse."

"I don't think things could have gotten any worse for Madison than finding out that the man she loved and was supposed to marry in two weeks turned out to be a total jerk."

"I am not a jerk," he said. "And I'm not perfect either. I made a mistake with Madison and I've regretted it ever since." He moved close to Holly and was glad to see that she didn't back away. "The one thing I've never regretted was meeting you."

Anderson ran his hand down the side of Holly's face and for a moment, she nearly gave in to its strength and warmth. But she was not about to dismiss this as merely an error in judgment. Didn't history have a way of repeating itself?

"Did you ever love Madison?" she asked.

"Yes, at one time."

"Were you in love with her when you pulled out of the marriage you asked for?"

Anderson shifted his eyes away from Holly's and then back again. "I loved her, but I was no longer *in love* with her."

Holly felt even more unsettled with his answer. Just how exactly did he define *love* and *in love?* And which way did he feel about her?

Sensing precisely what was going on in her head, Anderson said, "I'm *in love* with you, and I know the difference."

"Do you really?" she asked skeptically.

"Yeah, I do."

"When we made love, were you ever thinking about Madison?" Holly understood that a past relationship that had nearly turned into marriage must have had a strong sexual connection. She hated to think that he was comparing the two of them.

"I swear to you that I have never thought about her or any other woman when we've been intimate," Anderson said. "You've been more than enough to be my sole preoccupation."

"Why do I feel you used that line on Madison, too, at some point?"

"I haven't," he insisted. "Believe me when I tell you that I have no interest in anyone but you."

"Even if that were true, you can't run from your past, and I can't ignore it. Madison is my friend, and we can't just pretend she doesn't exist because that's more convenient for you."

Anderson's brows knitted. "So what are you saying?"

Holly met his gaze, steeling herself so she wouldn't give in to her impulses. "I'm saying that I can't do this right now. I think you should leave."

He took her hands, which were trembling. "Don't let something that's been over for two years ruin the good thing we've got going."

"I can't help the way I feel," she told him, removing her hands from his. "You need to work things out with Madison."

Anderson raised a brow. "Are you asking me to start a relationship with her again?"

Holly wasn't sure what she meant. She only knew that they needed to deal with their unresolved issues without her being caught squarely in the middle. She wondered if she was actually sending him back into the arms of a woman who may still be in love with him. But under the circumstances, it was a risk she had to take, even if it meant losing him for good.

"That's up to you," she said. "You can show yourself out."

Holly retreated to her bedroom and hoped he didn't follow her.

She waited until she heard the front door close before lying on the bed and trying to understand how their romance had suddenly come to a crashing halt.

Later that afternoon, Anderson sat in a tavern waiting for Lester to arrive. He could scarcely believe he suddenly found himself in this predicament. One moment he and Holly were exchanging kisses and declarations of love while feeding each other popcorn. The next, all hell broke loose as Madison showed up unexpectedly and caused chaos. Now he had been backed into a corner, his relationship with Holly was in jeopardy and damned if he knew what to do to save it.

What he did know was that whatever existed between him and Madison was over and there was nothing he could do to change that. *She hates my guts and maybe deservedly so,* he thought. How would talking to her make any difference or allow him to wipe the slate clean so he and Holly could get back together?

"You look like a man who's lost his best friend," Lester said as he walked up.

Anderson looked up. "Thanks for coming."

"How could I not? You made it sound pretty damned urgent."

"It is," Anderson said miserably.

Lester took a seat and poured beer from the pitcher into a mug while studying Anderson. "So what's up?"

Anderson tasted his own beer and wiped the foam from his mouth. He told Lester about Madison's unforeseen appearance at Holly's house and the chaos that followed.

"Oh, man," Lester said, shaking his head. "That must have really thrown you for a loop. Not to mention Holly and Madison."

"Tell me about it," Anderson said. "Things blew up in my face in a hurry."

"I'll bet. You had to know this would happen sooner or later. I mean, you and Madison still living in the same city, it was just a matter of time before you occupied the same space again."

"Yeah, but why now and why that space?" Anderson grumbled.

"Are you asking me that or yourself?" Lester tossed at him.

Anderson shrugged. "I don't know what the hell I'm saying or where to go from here."

"I think you do know where to go from here," Lester said.

Anderson eyed him. "Where's that?"

"Where else? To see Madison. You need to make things right with her."

"Yeah, and how do I do that without her trying to rip my head off?"

Lester chuckled. "I can't guarantee that she won't be out for blood. It's a risk you have to take, especially if you ever want to get past this and get back on Holly's good side."

Anderson conceded that Holly had pretty much said the same thing. But he wasn't sure that would solve anything, and it might even open up a new can of worms and cause things to truly spiral out of control. As if they could get any more out of control.

"I definitely want things back the way they were with Holly," he said. "I just don't see how reliving the past can—"

"Don't overthink this, just do it," Lester insisted. "You've asked for my advice as a friend and now I'm giving it to you. Remember, I'm the guy who was going to be your best man when you were supposed to marry Madison. Don't think I didn't hear what people were saying about how you went about ending the relationship. I figured you already had enough on your plate without hearing it from me. But now you're going to hear it. Get over yourself and make amends in any way you need to with her. I can't guarantee that it'll save your relationship with Holly, but it just might turn things around with Madison so that at least you can give her and yourself some sort of closure."

Anderson sat back and took a breath. He couldn't

outright reject his friend's words of wisdom. And he couldn't forget Holly's beauty and the love he felt for her. He had to own up to his past mistakes and hope Madison could somehow forgive him. And at the same time he had to let Holly know he was very serious about their relationship and would not give her up without a fight.

"All right," he told Lester. "I'll talk to her, assuming she'll let me."

"I think she will. My sense is that Madison just wants some answers so she can put this behind her, just like you'd like to." Lester leaned forward. "You've come a long way in your life since then. Now's the time to show her that."

"Yeah, I suppose you're right." Anderson was not about to run away from his troubles. Not anymore. If facing his demons was the way to get past them once and for all, he was game. Madison did deserve that much. He probably should have contacted her long ago to set things straight, but there never seemed like a good time. But there was no more putting it off.

Not when everything he'd built up with Holly was on the line. He had found in her the one thing that was missing in his life: a woman with whom he connected in every way. To lose that would be losing the best thing to ever happen to him. He would do whatever he had to do to prove his love to her.

Chapter 13

Two days later, Holly was already having second thoughts about kicking Anderson out of her house. But what other choice did she have? He had broken the heart of her friend Madison. How could she ignore that and continue her relationship with him? Especially since Madison had more or less given her an ultimatum: it was either her or Anderson.

Normally, Holly would never choose a female friend she had only recently met over a boyfriend whom she had fallen in love with. But this was far from a normal situation. It could well be some sort of sign that what had happened to Madison could happen to her. Did she really want to wait and find out? What if Anderson was simply a serial heartbreaker who either couldn't help himself or just didn't give a damn?

She had waited far too long for Mr. Right to wind up with Mr. Wrong, and she didn't think it was wise to disregard the clear warning signs.

Holly was still trying to battle the overpowering and conflicting feelings of love and desire she felt for Anderson when she walked into the Velvet Restaurant on Texas Street.

She saw Blythe sitting at a table, waving her in. Blythe stood when she got there and gave her a hug.

"I took the liberty of ordering us drinks, figuring you could use one about now," Blythe said.

"Yes, I could," Holly said as she sat down.

"That must have really thrown you for a loop to find out that Anderson had left a woman high and dry at the altar."

"It was definitely an eye opener," Holly said, tasting the cocktail. "These types of things just don't happen to me."

"Welcome to the real world," Blythe said, running fingers through her hair. "While my ex didn't exactly get cold feet before the wedding, he might as well have. He spent more time in bed with other women after we got married than with me."

Holly frowned. "Men can really be bastards sometimes."

"Yes, they can. But at least you got to see your man's true colors before you got too deeply wrapped up in him."

"The problem is, I am still deeply wrapped up in him," Holly admitted.

Blythe looked at her. "Don't tell me you're in love with Anderson."

"I wish I could say otherwise, but it's true. Falling out of love won't be easy, even if I have a very good reason for it."

"Maybe he's gotten it out of his system," Blythe said sympathetically. "If so, he might be worth keeping."

"Honestly, I'd like to believe that," Holly said, setting down her glass. "But do men who run away from commitments ever really change?"

"Some do, some don't. You have to decide which category Anderson fits in."

"As far as my friend Madison is concerned, he's a loser, plain and simple." Holly wrinkled her nose. "I hate the idea of a man coming between women. Unfortunately, Anderson has put me in an uncomfortable situation and he knows it."

"Life is all about uncomfortable situations. I've been in more than my fair share, both personally and professionally. That doesn't mean you necessarily have to turn and run. I'm sure your friend sees him as a dog, and maybe he is, but every circumstance is different. You can't let her feelings about Anderson become your own. I personally believe that women should never have to choose between a girlfriend and a boyfriend. That's not playing fair. If Anderson's half the man you thought you knew before this came out, you owe it to yourself to see this through and keep an open mind."

"Well put," Holly said. "Yes, I know people can grow up over time. But it's hard to fall for someone not knowing if he truly wants the same things I do in a relationship or if he'll back away the closer we become. I don't need someone like that in my life at this stage."

"Believe me, I hear you," Blythe said. "Been there, done that. You don't want to regret later something you can fix now." She tasted her drink. "At the end of the day, just go with your instincts and don't look back."

Holly smiled softly. "I'll try to remember that." The problem was that Holly's instincts told her one thing, but her common sense told her another. Would Madison's past become her future were she to continue her romance with Anderson? Or should she not set her sights too high and simply enjoy what she and Anderson had while they had it?

It was an issue that Holly didn't expect to resolve overnight, given that her heart still belonged to Anderson.

Anderson was tentative for a moment before he pressed the dial button for Madison's number that was still saved in his cell phone. He wouldn't be too surprised if she had changed her phone number after the way their relationship had ended. But she answered after two rings.

"Hey, it's Anderson," he said.

She waited a long moment before saying flatly, "Hi."

"Can we meet?"

Another pause. "Not sure there's anything to talk about."

"I think there is," Anderson said, twirling a pen as he

sat at his desk. "At least there are some things I'd like to say if you'd give me the chance. Please…"

Madison sighed. "All right. When and where?"

"How about noon at the Cedar Bistro on—"

"I know where it is." She cut him off. "As you may recall, we used to go there quite a bit."

"I remember," he said quietly. He had chosen the spot as a means to break the ice. "So I'll see you then?"

"Fine."

Madison hung up and Anderson was left to wonder if this was a good idea. Nevertheless, he had to follow through and hope for the best. If he was going to get back in Holly's good graces, he needed to square things with Madison.

He asked his assistant to clear his afternoon schedule, since he didn't know how long this would take. Though he missed Holly like hell, he resisted calling her till he had a chance to speak with Madison.

Anderson drove to the bistro and was already at the table by the time Madison got there. She looked gorgeous in an attractive pink blouse and brown pencil skirt.

"Hi," he said, standing up. "Thanks for coming."

"I nearly didn't, but decided to see what you had to say."

He waited for her to sit and then did the same. "Can I get you something to drink?"

"Water will be fine," she said, and sipped some that had already been poured in a glass.

Anderson tasted the wine he'd ordered. "You look great," he said sincerely.

"Is that why you called off the wedding—because I look so great?"

She was angry and wasn't holding back, and he had to respect that. "It goes a lot deeper than that."

"So tell me."

Anderson wondered how best to say this without causing her to get up and leave. "First of all, I'm sorry about everything. I really wish I had done things differently, but I was at a different place then."

Madison frowned. "I was under the impression we were in the same place."

"We weren't," he said. "I was career driven, self-centered and a little too full of myself."

She batted her eyes. "And I'm supposed to believe you've changed?"

"I have changed."

"You look exactly the same to me," she said, her words laced with sarcasm.

"I've changed inside," he told her. "I'm a better person today, more into giving than receiving, and trying to lead a less stressful life."

"That's nice and all, but it doesn't tell me anything about why you led me on only to drop me two weeks before our wedding," Madison argued.

Anderson sipped his wine thoughtfully. "I thought it was the best thing to do at the time."

Her eyes narrowed. "Best for whom? Certainly not me."

He paused. "We were fighting."

"All couples do," she said. "You don't call off your wedding because of that."

"Maybe more people should," he said. "My point is that between us having our issues and my striving to get ahead in my career, I just felt I wasn't ready for marriage. I know I should have come directly to you with this instead of telling you over the phone, but at the time it seemed like an easier way for you to digest than if we were face-to-face."

Madison sucked in a deep breath. "I think I will have that drink now."

Anderson ordered it and a refill for himself, while his difficult words sank in. He wasn't sure if she would let him have it or what.

"You deserved better," he said tonelessly.

"I had the best," she countered. "Or at least I thought so at the time."

Anderson grimaced. "We were just better off as friends."

Madison tasted her drink pensively. "So are you in love with Holly?"

"Yeah, I am."

"And I take it she loves you?"

"I think so, though I'm not sure how she feels at this point," he said.

"Probably confused, just like I am." Madison gave him a hard look. "Did you ever truly love me? Or was it all about sex and then you just had to back out when the pressure was on?"

Anderson sat back. "It was never just about sex with you. Yes, I did love you at one time, but—"

"But what? It wasn't strong enough to survive cold feet?"

"It wasn't strong enough to survive my gut instincts that we weren't right for each other," he responded. "I never wanted to hurt you, but I really believed that it would have been much worse had we gone through with the wedding."

"Maybe it would have been," she conceded. "Especially if you weren't prepared to give me the same unconditional love I had for you."

Anderson remained mute, his silence speaking louder than any words he could possibly say. He wondered if she had been able to move on to a new relationship. Or had she been carrying a bitter pill around all this time?

"I'll always care for you and wish you the best in life. I mean that," he said.

"As long as that life isn't with you," Madison said evenly.

Anderson looked at her. "We're better off as friends," he repeated, "if that's possible."

She licked her lips. "Maybe someday. Right now, it's still too recent for any kind of reconnection."

"I understand," he said.

She met his gaze. "Are you planning to ask Holly to marry you?"

He took a breath on that one. Yes, he did love her and marriage was a possibility, if they were even still a couple. But before he ever went that route again, he wanted to know in his heart of hearts that he was mentally prepared to see it through.

"We haven't gotten that far in our relationship," he said truthfully.

"Well, my advice to you is to never put her or any other woman through the hell you put me through."

"I don't intend to," Anderson promised.

"Hope you mean it," Madison said, eyeing him narrowly. "I like Holly and she deserves to be with someone who wants the same things she does. And I believe that includes having a man who won't run from her when the going gets tough."

"I get it." Anderson finished off his drink. He was trying to maintain his cool even when it hurt to be reminded of how he'd screwed things up with Madison. He wondered if Holly was looking for marriage and, if so, if she could still see him as marriage material at this point.

It was something that would weigh heavily on his mind until he spoke to her.

Chapter 14

"We sure do know how to pick them, sis," Stuart said to Holly in a video chat.

"Do we ever," Holly said humorlessly as she sat in the den at her father's house. "How could I know that Anderson wasn't the marrying type?"

"You couldn't have known—not if he didn't bother telling you while he knew you were starting to have feelings for him. Some men play that game and women tend to fall for it."

Holly wished she could say she hadn't fallen for Anderson's charms. But that would be a lie. The man had allowed her to fall in love with him. Now what was she supposed to do with that? Yes, the sex was wonderful and the companionship was, too. But deep down inside she had been hoping for more at the end of the day. Apparently they weren't on the same page with that.

"Guilty as charged," she admitted sadly.

"Obviously your friend Madison was a victim, too," Stuart said.

"She's dealing with it." Holly wasn't sure just how well at the moment, but she believed Madison would find a way to move past her issues with Anderson.

"That's good anyway. She seems like a nice woman who deserved better," Stuart said.

"You could always move back to Houston and cheer her up," Holly quipped, knowing that wasn't about to happen anytime soon. He seemed to have really found himself in the laid-back, friendly atmosphere of Portland.

"Thanks, but no thanks," Stuart said with a chuckle. "I'll leave the cheering up to some other lucky man who may cross her path there. Assuming she's able to get Anderson out of her head."

It was clear to Holly that Stuart was also referring to his own failed marriage and how that had been difficult to get past. He also deserved to be happy with a woman who would love him and his daughters to death and not abandon them.

"I had to try," Holly said, knowing it would have been good for their father and her if Stuart and the girls lived in Houston.

"And I commend you for that," he told her, grinning. "Right now I'm too focused on writing my next novel and, of course, keeping Dottie and Carrie from ripping each other's hair out to think about romance. You, on the other hand, should really forget all about Anderson and find yourself a stand-up guy who wants the same things you do in a relationship."

Holly frowned. "I thought that guy was Anderson."

"Apparently you thought wrong."

"Apparently." She sat back in the chair. "You know me too well."

Stuart smiled. "Of course, I'm your big brother. Trust me when I say that you'll get past this and move on."

"You mean like you have?" she couldn't help but say.

"We're not talking about me."

"Maybe we should be," Holly said.

"Uh-oh," Stuart said, "looks like the girls need their daddy again. We'll pick up this conversation later."

"Yeah, right," Holly said, laughing. "Blame it on your daughters for ducking out on me."

Stuart smiled. "You just wait till you have kids someday and you'll see that they can keep you going day and night."

"I know," Holly said. "I'm just playing with you. Give them my love and I'll talk to you later."

"I will. Say hello to Dad for me. 'Bye."

Holly watched the little screen go blank. In spite of everything, she felt a little better after talking to Stuart. But what came next for her? Was Anderson still someone she should be interested in? Or was this a clear sign that she needed to look elsewhere for a committed relationship?

She went to find her father, who was in the kitchen cooking. This had become a favorite pastime of his since he retired.

"How's your brother?" he asked as he peeled potatoes.

"Being his usual self. Giving plenty of advice, but not taking any."

Robert smiled. "Sounds like someone else I know."

Holly batted her lashes. "Who, me?"

"Well, you two are cut from the same cloth," he said. "You got that from your mother, not me."

Holly couldn't help but laugh. "I think it's more the other way around. Anyway, since when have I not taken your advice?"

He scratched his head. "Well, I did suggest that you not write off Anderson just yet."

"Who says I have?" she asked.

"I can tell what's going on in that head of yours. Yeah, I know he did Madison wrong and all that, but it doesn't mean you're headed down the same path."

"No one said anything about the same path, if you're talking about getting married," Holly said, rolling her eyes. Quite frankly, that was the last thing on her mind right now.

"All I'm saying is to give this thing a chance with the man and see how it goes," Robert said, checking a pot on the stove. "Maybe you're the one for him and she wasn't—did you ever think about that?"

How could she not think about it, given the passion she had experienced with Anderson that made her feel more alive than she ever had before. Not to mention that he had certainly given her the strong impression that she meant something real and very special to him. Could he really have just been stringing her along?

Holly decided to evade the conversation, since she was unwilling to say one way or the other where things were headed between her and Anderson, especially when she didn't have a clue at this point. Also, she wasn't sure she wanted to be the woman he ended up with after Madison, knowing her friend was still hurting.

How would I feel were the situation reversed? she wondered. All she could do was try to keep an open mind and see where things were headed with Anderson, if anywhere.

The following day, Holly got a call from Anderson asking if he could drop by her place to talk. She agreed—she realized that avoiding him wouldn't solve anything even though she wasn't sure just how much talking would accomplish either. The facts wouldn't change, no matter how much Anderson tried to extricate himself from his tight spot.

Still, Holly felt she owed it to herself to hear him out before deciding if what they had was worth holding on to.

When Anderson arrived, dressed casually and looking very sexy, Holly nearly jumped into his arms instinctively. But she checked herself, not willing to succumb to carnal instincts over common sense.

"Hey," Anderson said.

"Hi." Holly kept her voice level as though they were merely acquaintances rather than lovers. She touched her top and then jeans, as if to do something with her hands, before waving him inside.

Anderson almost felt as if he was there for the first time.

"How have you been?" he asked Holly, since her eyes were unreadable.

"I've definitely been better." She gave him an honest reply. "Learning that my boyfriend broke off an engagement with my friend is still sinking in."

Anderson swallowed thickly. At least she hadn't rejected him outright, which he considered to be a good sign. "Mind if we sit down?" he asked.

"No." In fact, Holly thought that, with her wobbly knees, sitting was precisely the thing to do.

They sat on the couch just as they were when Madison showed up last week. Only this time the atmosphere was decidedly cooler.

Anderson eyed Holly, noting that she was sitting farther away from him than he wanted. He respected that and understood he had to win her back.

"I went to see Madison," he said.

"And?"

"We talked. I owned up to the mistakes I made in ending our relationship."

Holly considered that a start, at least. "How did she take it?"

"She held up," Anderson said, leaning back. "I never

wanted to hurt Madison and, deep down, I think she understands that. Things were not perfect between us when we were involved, but we kind of swept it under the rug as if everything would work itself out once we said 'I do.' It definitely played a big role in my wanting out, as did my own misguided priorities at the time."

Holly wondered if he expected every relationship to be utterly perfect and wanted out if it ever fell short of that. "What kind of problems were you having?" she asked.

"Well, Madison and I often fought about silly little things, such as where to go or what to do, or how I spent my time when I wasn't with her."

"That's normal," Holly said.

"Maybe, but too much got to be a drag." He sighed. "There were also some bigger disagreements, such as the trust issue. She feared that I might cheat on her and wasn't afraid to tell me about her suspicions."

Holly met his eyes. "Did she have reason to feel that way?"

"None whatsoever," he said. "As I've told you before, I never stray from the woman I am involved with. Madison didn't always get that. Apparently some guy she used to date was a player, which made it harder for her to accept that other men were nothing like that."

Holly had also wanted to stay away from men who only wanted to sleep with as many women as possible. Instinctively, she believed Anderson was not that type of man. But he had still broken Madison's heart in a way no woman would ever want to go through.

"Why didn't you simply communicate your feelings to Madison about this up front, instead of leading her to believe you wanted the marriage as much as she did?"

Anderson sighed. It wasn't easy reliving the past, even with someone he hoped would be part of his future. But he would do whatever it took to get them beyond this.

"The truth is that I thought at the time I did want to marry her," he said. "But something still didn't seem right about us tying the knot—be it my ambitious agenda as an attorney, or my immaturity at the time or my feeling that we just weren't meant to be husband and wife. As far as communicating my feelings goes, I think I did often enough. Only, Madison didn't always listen."

Holly knew that not all couples listened to each other when it came to what they wanted and didn't want in a relationship. And sometimes it came down to one side or the other taking drastic measures to shake up things. In this case, it was Anderson who had made the bold move to walk away from Madison. *Can I really fault him for preventing what seemed like a disaster waiting to happen?* Holly asked herself.

She gazed at him. "So where do things stand now with you and Madison?"

Anderson stared in response to the question. "We got things out in the open," he said. "I think she has a better understanding of why I did things the way I did and is ready to put closure to it."

"I hope so," Holly said. The last thing she wanted was for Madison to keep this bottled up inside her forever, preventing another man from getting inside the barrier.

Anderson inched closer to Holly. "What about us?"

Holly's pulse raced at the thought of them together. But there was still the fear that he wasn't looking for a long-term commitment.

"You tell me," she responded. "What is it *you* really want in this relationship?"

"I want you and only you to be my lady, and I'm not going anywhere."

Those were words that registered with Holly. But could she trust him to stand behind them? Or would opening her heart to him again leave her vulnerable to a letdown?

"I want to believe that," she said.

He took her hand. "You can," he said. "I'm not the person I was two years ago. I have a better understanding of what works for me and what I want in a girlfriend." He kissed her hand. "And that's you."

Holly practically melted as much from his heartfelt words as from the power of his touch. Yet she still remained guarded. "Let's just take it one day at a time and see what happens," she said.

Anderson smiled. "I can live with that."

He leaned forward, wanting badly to seal things with a kiss. Tilting his head, Anderson gently put his mouth to Holly's lips. When she showed no indication of being put off by it, he moved in for a deeper kiss. She reciprocated, widening her mouth and drawing him in.

Holly abandoned any resistance she felt the moment their mouths connected. She was unable to deny how much she missed his kisses, his scent, his closeness and his presence. She wrapped her hands around his head, and they kissed passionately as her libido rose to a fever pitch.

Anderson caressed her tautened nipples, causing an ache between her legs, and she teased his hard erection through his pants. After what seemed like an endless kiss, they took their passion to the bedroom.

Stripping naked, Anderson slipped on a condom and lowered himself onto Holly's waiting body. He entered her deeply, moaning from the pleasurable tightness surrounding him. Her legs were wrapped high around his back and their bodies began to rock up and down as they made love lustfully.

Holly conquered Anderson's head, face, chin and finally his mouth with her fervent kisses, slipping her tongue inside his lips. Her back arched off the bed and her breasts heaved as he propelled himself into her time and time again and as she received his mighty thrusts with ecstasy. When her orgasm came, Holly cried out, knowing it was as much music to his ears as it was hers. Her moist body quivered intensely and she rode the sensations as far as they would take her.

Anderson exploded with fire inside Holly. His mind, body and soul worked in unison as Holly brought about this powerful release. His grunts and gasps left him breathless, but he continued to enjoy the moment. Their spent bodies were close together, and the scent of sex filled the air with satisfaction.

Afterward they held each other, content knowing they had overcome a major hurdle.

Chapter 15

On Saturday, Holly left work and headed for a club after Madison asked to meet her there. Holly was happy to hear from her and a little nervous at the same time. Would Madison scold her for not breaking things off with Anderson for good? Or would they agree to disagree on Anderson's character?

Holly had not quite put Anderson's failed relationship with Madison behind her, even though she had resumed her own relationship with him. She had no idea where they were headed, but felt she owed it to herself to enjoy the present. Holly also hoped that Madison still wanted to maintain their friendship.

Inside the club, Holly spotted Madison, who was coming toward her.

"Hey, girl," Holly said, hoping to break the ice right away.

"Hi there," Madison said. "Glad you could make it."

Holly smiled. "I was happy to hear from you."

"I got us a table," Madison told her.

Holly followed her toward the middle of the club and ordered margaritas.

"First of all, I want to apologize for putting you on the spot last week," Madison said, smoothing an eyebrow. "I should never have reacted that way with you."

"No apology necessary," Holly said sincerely. "Who could blame you for something you didn't see coming till it was too late?"

"I know, but we're friends and it certainly wasn't your fault that you happened to be dating my ex."

"How are you doing?" Holly wanted to know.

"Better now," Madison said. "I suppose Anderson told you that we talked."

Holly nodded. "Yes, he did without going into too much detail, other than that you tried to work out your differences."

"Something like that."

The drinks arrived and Madison insisted on paying for them.

Holly tasted her drink, curious to see where things now stood between Madison and Anderson.

Madison sipped the margarita before saying, "It was an interesting conversation. I'll be honest when I tell you that I carried bitterness with me for a long time and wanted to hate Anderson for calling off our wedding. But you know what? I've come to realize that's not a healthy way to process things. After talking to Anderson, I'm ready to put it behind me and move on with my life."

"That's great to hear," Holly said.

"Don't get me wrong, I'll never be able to erase the memory of being told by the man you thought you were going to marry that he was calling it off and there wasn't a damned thing you could do about it." Madison sighed. "However, I have to face up to the fact that it wasn't entirely his fault. We did have some issues at the time that I chose to ignore more than he did, I guess. In any event, maybe we just weren't meant to be, and I have to accept it."

"I'm really sorry that things didn't work out for you two," Holly said.

"Don't be," Madison said, licking her lips. "We had our day and there were some good times, but they just didn't last. I hope it's different with you."

"We're just taking it slow right now." Holly rested her arms on the table. She didn't want Madison to think they were already making wedding plans, since that definitely wasn't in the cards at this stage.

"Good for you. It's definitely important that you make sure you're completely on the same page before getting too caught up in something that doesn't work out the way it was intended to."

"I agree," Holly said. "So do you think Anderson's incapable of ever settling down with a woman?" *Might as well see if the voice of experience believes he's a losing cause,* she thought.

"If you're asking me if I think he'll get cold feet before a wedding ever occurs, the honest answer is that I just don't know. He swears he's a changed man. I could say a zebra never changes it stripes, but maybe this one has. That will be for you to establish if that's where your relationship is headed."

"I'd love to get married someday," Holly admitted. "And, yes, I could see Anderson as a husband. But since I'm not sure he will ever see himself that way, I think it's best not to look that far ahead and just enjoy each other's company right now."

"Probably a smart way to look at it," Madison said.

"And what about you? Are you back in the market for a man?" Holly asked hopefully.

Madison chuckled. "Yes, I am. But I'm not holding my breath waiting."

"Hey, there are a lot of good men in Houston," Holly said.

"I don't doubt it, even if they have been hard to come by in my life. Must be I'm looking in all the wrong places."

"So start checking out the right places," Holly told her.

Madison laughed. "I hope to do that with a fresh start. I'm moving…"

"Moving?" Holly's eyes widened.

"Yes, I've been thinking about it for a while now.

This seems as good a time as any to put my bad memories in Houston behind me and go somewhere else."

"But where will you go?" Holly paid for a second round of drinks as she considered where Madison might move. "Dallas? San Antonio?"

"I'm moving to Portland," Madison said.

"Portland, Oregon? Of all places?"

Madison nodded. "I was offered a job there as a senior book reviewer for an upscale magazine with a strong internet presence. So I said, hey, why not?"

"I couldn't agree more," Holly said. "You will love the Rose City, as Portland is called, with all its nature."

"It sounds wonderful," Madison said.

"And the city is known for its popularity with bicyclists, so you'll fit right in."

"That's good to know."

"I'm sure my brother would be happy to show you around," Holly said.

Madison smiled. "I'd like that."

Holly was already imagining the two of them hitting it off. Though she recalled Madison saying she wasn't very good with children, Holly believed she would warm up to Carrie and Dottie in a hurry.

"That would also give me another reason to visit Portland," Holly added.

"Come any time you like," Madison told her. "For the time being, you'll have to put up with me being your friend and neighbor in Houston. Hope you don't feel it's too awkward with us continuing to hang out."

"I don't," Holly assured her. "We're friends and nothing has to change."

"Good. If Anderson has a problem with it, that's for him to deal with," Madison said.

Holly laughed. "I feel the same way." She didn't think it would be an issue with him anyway.

Her thoughts turned to the romance she had with Anderson. Lately, it had been hotter than ever, full of sweet whispers of love to one another. Was that an indication that they might eventually have the type of lasting relationship that had fallen short between him and Madison?

Or was she merely deluding herself into seeing more than what was actually there?

Anderson was at the gym working out with Lester. He had brought his friend up to date on where things stood with Madison and Holly. As far as Anderson was concerned, he had dodged a bullet or two with the whole situation.

"Well, it looks like things just might work out for you after all, buddy," Lester said, as he lifted weights.

"That's the hope," Anderson said.

"Just think if you had reached out to Madison way back when, you could have saved yourself a lot of grief."

"Something tells me that Madison wasn't in any mood to talk about things before now," Anderson said, wiping his brow. "And, frankly, neither was I. We both had some growing up to do, maybe me more than her."

"I agree," Lester said. "So now you're all grown up and you've turned your attention to Holly."

"Yeah, I have." The thought of the last time they made love hit Anderson, causing him to check the unbridled desire he had for Holly. Now that they were back on track, he couldn't imagine not having her as an integral part of his life.

Lester looked up at him. "And how do you plan to handle things this time around?"

"Meaning…?"

"You love her, right?"

"Yeah, definitely."

"I assume from all the sparks flying between you two that the feeling is mutual?"

Anderson nodded. "She's told me as much on more than one occasion."

"So the question that begs to be answered is when do you plan to put a ring on her finger? And don't tell me the thought has never entered your mind."

A half grin played on Anderson's lips. How could he not have considered marrying Holly? Especially given the way he felt about her. She would make the perfect wife for him. But was this the right time to go there? Or would it be a mistake to make his move too soon?

"I've thought about it," he said.

"And what did you come up with?" Lester asked eagerly.

Anderson sighed. "I want Holly to be my wife," he stressed. "However, bringing that up this soon to when she found out about my mishap with Madison sounds like a disaster waiting to happen. I'd rather put some distance there and prove to Holly just how much she means to me before popping the question."

"Hmm…yeah, I suppose that makes sense." Lester did some stretching. "As long as you don't wait too long to make your move."

"I don't intend to," Anderson said.

"Good, because women won't wait forever to get a ring. Take it from someone who knows from experience—twice. In the case of Holly, the last thing she wants is to have reason to believe that you'll always have cold feet. It could cause her to pull away and look elsewhere."

"I won't let that happen," Anderson insisted, running a towel across his perspiring head and face. "She means too much to me to let her get away."

"That's what I want to hear," Lester said. "Besides, since you were once my best man, I've been waiting ever since for a little quid pro quo."

Anderson smiled. "When it happens, you can count on being my best man."

Lester smiled. "Cool."

Anderson shook his friend's hand and headed for the shower. The thought of redeeming himself with a second marriage proposal was still on his mind, and he wondered if Holly would ever agree to be his bride.

Chapter 16

In early November, Holly spent the night at Anderson's place, basking in the intensity of their lovemaking and the connection that kept them in sync every step of the way. They had fallen asleep in each other's arms in the wee hours of the morning, which was the last thing Holly remembered before hearing the words "Wake up, sleepyhead—"

She opened her eyes and saw Anderson standing there with a tray in his hands. "What's this?" she asked, adjusting her eyes to the daylight.

"It's called breakfast in bed," he said, grinning. "Waffles with real maple syrup, bacon, scrambled eggs, orange juice and coffee."

"You didn't have to…" she began.

"I was happy to serve my beautiful lady. Especially when she looks sexy as hell in a nightshirt in my bed." Anderson checked his libido, feeling that now was not the time to jump her bones, appealing as they were. He set the tray on her lap.

"Why, thank you." Holly could barely remember putting on the nightshirt. She had been naked, as was he, when they went to bed. She inhaled the scent of food. "Smells good."

"It will taste even better," he promised. "I'll even feed you, if you like."

She smiled, tempted. "That's so sweet, but I'll try it on my own first." She grabbed a slice of bacon and bit off a piece, then held it up to his mouth. "I don't mind feeding you, though."

Anderson bit into the bacon. "And I don't mind your doing it either." He loved looking at her in the morning, noon or night, as she was always a gorgeous sight. "But I'd rather watch you eat."

"Where's your food?" she asked.

"I already finished it while you were sound asleep. I chose not to disturb your snoozing."

"How thoughtful of you." She sliced into the waffle, wondering how she got so lucky.

"What can I say, you bring out the best in me," he said, smiling.

"Or worst," she said naughtily, remembering their red-hot sex in the night.

Anderson read her mind. "That too." Fresh thoughts tickled his libido. "Maybe after breakfast, we can—"

Holly licked her lips invitingly. "I don't see why not." She wondered if there would ever come a day when she could get enough of him.

A week later, Holly talked Anderson into going bike riding with her. She considered it a triumph to get him out of the gym for some outdoor exercise.

"Are you sure you can keep up with me?" she teased him.

"I think I can manage," Anderson said. He had only ridden a bicycle sporadically over the years. But now, with Holly's prompting, he planned to ride regularly with her. In turn, he intended to get her to the gym for some workouts.

They rode on the quiet streets near Holly's house and at the nearby park. She was only mildly surprised that Anderson seemed to have little trouble staying with her and even occasionally forcing her to catch up to him. It appeared as though she had met her match in bicycling, just as she had in bed. She wondered if this compatibility would know no bounds as their relationship continued to prosper.

Anderson got as much of a thrill from watching Holly ride with such grace and athleticism as he did working on his cardio. This seemed as good a time as any to throw something at her that he had been thinking about.

"How would you feel about us living together?" It seemed like a good first step in their evolving relationship.

Holly was taken aback by the question.

"I don't know," she told him honestly. "What do you think about it?"

Anderson sighed, not wanting to say the wrong thing. "I think it would be a good thing for us. We wouldn't have to go back and forth between our places and we'd always be there to fall asleep and wake up together."

"That sounds nice," Holly said, feeling the strain in her legs from pedaling. "I'm not really sure, though, if I'm ready to give up my own space. And where would you want to live—your place or mine?"

"Either one," Anderson said, his heart beating fast. "I have no problem living with you or having you move into my place. We could even consider moving somewhere new together."

Holly was a bit disappointed that there was no talk of marriage in the equation. Or was that a blessing in disguise, considering his track record? Was this his way of having a committed relationship minus the official piece of paper?

"Why not ask me to marry you?" she asked bluntly. "Or are you still struggling with the idea of having a wife instead of a lover?"

Anderson sucked in a deep breath. "This isn't about Madison or our past situation," he said flatly. "I just thought this would be best for both of us at this point."

"I'm not sure it is," Holly said candidly. "Living with someone is a serious thing for me. It means sacrificing my independence with no guarantees that it will last."

He held her gaze. "And you think marriage is a guarantee?"

"No, it isn't," she admitted. "But it would show me that we're entering into a life together the right way—at least the way my parents did it. Their values in that regard were passed down to me."

"I can understand that," Anderson said. "I wasn't suggesting that this would be forever. Marriage can still come later. I just see no reason for us to go there right now when things are going so well, though."

"If that's true, why rock the boat by living together at all?" she challenged him. "Unless you simply have something against marriage that will always be there, no matter how long we're together."

Anderson's brows bridged. He had dug a hole for himself that threatened to get deeper if he wasn't careful. "I have nothing against marriage," he said. "This has nothing to do with Madison and—"

"Are you sure about that?" Holly questioned. "Because it sounds to me like you're trying to convince yourself. If you don't want to marry me, just say so and I'll deal with it. I just don't want to play games like living together and expecting something that never materializes."

"I'm sorry if the idea of living together has put you off." He sighed, feeling he had bitten off more than he could chew. "It definitely wasn't a game to me, but an honest effort to spend more of our free time together. As for marrying you, it is something I think about and want to do when the time is right for both of us."

"Well, when it is, you let me know," she said tersely. "In the meantime, I don't think living together will cut it for me. I'm sorry."

"Don't be," he insisted. "It was just a thought. Let's keep things as they are, if that's okay with you."

Was it? Holly wondered if this had touched upon a nerve that would make it impossible for her to be happy with the way things were. Or was she putting undue pressure on him to do what he obviously wasn't comfortable doing?

The last thing she wanted was to marry someone who only agreed to be her husband to please her and not himself. Was that what Madison would have gotten had they tied the knot?

I have to be real about this and not try to push him, Holly thought as they neared her house. They had a good thing going and she should just enjoy it for what it was.

"Things are fine the way they are," she finally told Anderson. But deep down inside, she had reservations about that.

"That's good to know." Anderson smiled thinly at her. He realized that he had work to do to keep her happy and sustain their relationship.

On Thanksgiving, Anderson and Holly spent the afternoon at the soup kitchen, feeding the hungry.

"I'm so glad you were both able to give of yourselves on this special day," Esther told them during a break.

"It was the right thing to do," Anderson said.

"I agree," Holly said, smiling. "It's a wonderful way to help the less fortunate."

"You two make a great team," Esther said in a bubbly tone. "Anderson, you better not let this lovely young woman get away. Otherwise you'll have to answer to me."

"I wouldn't want to have to do that." He chuckled. "I have no intention of letting her get away." Not if it was within his power to keep them together as a couple. Anderson believed Holly was of the same mind. They seemed to have settled into their relationship and had agreed to leave the future open.

A few minutes later, they were back to feeding people turkey and dressing, mashed potatoes, corn bread, green beans and carrot cake.

"Happy Thanksgiving," Holly said. She greeted everyone she served warmly, and she was grateful for her own blessings and grateful that Anderson had given her this opportunity to do even more to help others.

"You're getting really good at this," Anderson whispered in her ear. "And starting to grow on Esther."

"I'll take both as compliments," she told him softly. "I'm sure you can find ways later to show your real appreciation."

He grinned. "Count on it." Anderson plopped a generous portion of dressing on the plate before him. He imagined that dressing was probably also on the menu for tonight's Thanksgiving dinner that Holly's father had invited them over to share. Anderson welcomed another opportunity to bond with him and to show

Holly that he was in this relationship for the long haul, whether they had a marriage certificate or not.

Holly helped her father by setting the table and pouring the drinks, since he had stubbornly insisted on cooking the Thanksgiving meal all by himself. She suspected he wanted to impress Anderson, who had talked about football with him earlier and seemed to have won her father over.

It meant a lot to Holly to have the two current men in her life get along. That still didn't tell her if she could be content in a relationship that didn't include marriage. Or, for that matter, if asking for more would simply push Anderson away.

Anderson stuffed himself with the huge meal prepared by Holly's father, which included roast beef, corn-bread dressing, macaroni and cheese, greens and biscuits.

"Now I know where Holly got her cooking skills," he said as they sat at the dining room table.

"Thanks," Robert said with a laugh. "Actually, the inheritance would have to come from her mother, who taught her and I much of what we know about cooking."

"Then I applaud both of your parents," Anderson said, looking at Holly. "I'm sure your mother would have approved of this meal."

"I'm sure she would have, too." Holly smiled as she dabbed a napkin at the corners of her mouth. She was certain her mother would have approved of him, too, though she would have expected them to get married sooner rather than later.

"So Holly tells me you're trying to find your father," Robert said, biting into a biscuit.

Anderson nodded. "Yeah, I owe her for pushing me to do it."

"How's that working out for you?"

"A private detective is still looking for him," Anderson said. "It's probably a long shot, but I haven't given up."

"I really hope it works out for you," Robert said. "Family is important, even if they're distant."

"I'm sure you're right." Truthfully, Anderson was still reserving judgment about that. He had survived well without a father and didn't necessarily need one at this stage of his life. But should he materialize and be willing to meet him, why not see how it went?

Holly got to her feet. "I'll clear the table," she said.

"I can help," offered Anderson.

"That won't be necessary. You and Dad can catch some of the football game that's on tonight."

"Good idea," Robert said, getting up and stretching his legs. "The Texans aren't playing, but I still love to watch a game."

"Ditto," Anderson said. He stood up, grinning. He suspected that Holly wanted him to spend some alone time with her father for perhaps some more interrogation.

They went to the den, where the big-screen television was already on. The game was tied early in the third quarter.

Anderson sat in a chair after Robert made himself comfortable on a recliner.

"It seems like my daughter has become quite fond of you," he said. "I think this is the longest time she's ever dated anyone."

"I'm very fond of her, too," Anderson said.

"I'm glad to know that. Where do you see your relationship with Holly going?"

Anderson sat back, and appeared deep in thought. "I'm in love with your daughter," he said.

"I gathered as much," Robert said. "And it's clear that she feels the same way about you."

"I want to make her happy—whether we date long-term or get married."

Robert faced him. "I understand you had some marital issues before."

"Yeah," Anderson conceded, figuring he knew all the details. "I'm trying not to make the mistakes of the past. I want to do what's right today, whatever that may be."

"That's a good attitude to have. I just don't want Holly to get hurt along the way."

"Neither do I," Anderson said sincerely. "I will always be straight with her. I'd like to see if we can figure out every step we take together."

"Sounds fair enough." Robert tugged at his chin. "That's all I have to say about it. I wish you and Holly well."

"Thank you." Anderson grinned, happy to have her father in his corner.

He heard Holly coming in behind him. "Did I miss anything?" she asked.

Anderson turned to the television and smiled. "Afraid so," he said, assuming Robert would fill her in on their conversation. "San Francisco just scored again to take the lead."

Chapter 17

In December, Holly was on the set finishing a news segment about this year's KOEN toy drive. "Along with many of my colleagues, I will be at Coral Square all day tomorrow collecting new unwrapped toys for children. Please do your part to help make this Christmas one that lights the faces of as many children as possible. I look forward to seeing you, shaking your hand and thanking you for your generosity. Have a good day…"

"You sure convinced me to show up with toys for the kiddies," Anderson joked. He had come to the station to watch her do her thing. They were planning to go out to a jazz supper club afterward with Lester and his wife.

Holly poked his chest playfully. "Somehow I don't think it would have taken much to win you over, mister."

"True, since you do that every time." He kissed her on the lips, not particularly caring if anyone saw them. After all, his very brief employment there had ended some time ago.

"I don't know about that," she said, using a finger to wipe lipstick from his mouth, "but it sounds good anyway."

"Are we ready to head out?" he asked.

"Yes, let me just grab my purse from my dressing room."

Holly was happy to be seen at the studio with her handsome man. She checked her reflection in the mirror and was satisfied with what she saw. Nonetheless, she applied a little lip gloss, brushed her hair and dabbed on some Oscar de la Renta perfume. Her gray blazer and matching skirt went well with a silk, rose-colored V-neck blouse and low-heeled black pumps. Though this was one of her work outfits, she was sure it would suffice for having dinner and listening to some jazz music with Anderson's friends.

Anderson was holding Holly's hand when they walked inside the Satin Jazz Supper Club. They were greeted right away by Lester and his wife, Odette, then Lester introduced her to Holly.

"Nice to finally meet you," Odette said, "since Lester has practically bragged about knowing Anderson's anchorwoman girlfriend."

Holly blushed, gazing at the petite, thirtysomething

woman with short black curly hair and bangs. "You too," she told her.

"Let's get ourselves a table and check out a performance that is straight from another era," Lester said.

"I can hardly wait," Anderson said.

They sat and ordered their meals and cocktails.

"So what's it like doing the news?" Odette peered at Holly as she sipped her drink.

Holly smiled; she was used to such questions. "When I first started in the business, I was a bundle of nerves every time I went before the camera. Now it's pretty routine. I just read the script and improvise where necessary."

"Must be fun being on television," Odette said.

"I wouldn't exactly call it fun," Holly said, sipping her cocktail. "It's just a job like any other, except it happens to show up on people's television screens."

"See, I told you," Lester said, chuckling. "Anderson's latched onto someone who's completely down-to-earth."

Anderson grinned. "Yeah, Holly's as modest as she is beautiful."

Holly blushed, not expecting all the attention directed toward her. She had always just wanted a private life, even though she enjoyed working in broadcast journalism. With Anderson, she had found a man who treated her like an equal, which was the same way she viewed him.

"Thanks, everyone," she said, looking at the stage, "but I'm not the center of attention. She is—"

The shapely vocalist wearing a purple rhinestone-pleated gown was belting out a song with a voice that reminded Holly of a cross between Ella Fitzgerald and Sarah Vaughan, two of her favorite jazz singers.

Anderson was inclined to agree with Holly. He wrapped his arm around her as they watched the performer woo the audience. "She's definitely got it going on," he said. Just as Holly did in ways that went well beyond the surface. Loving her was the best thing he had going for him, and he was beginning to realize that more and more with each passing day.

During a break in the music, Anderson and Lester were left alone while the ladies went to freshen up.

"They seem to be getting along well," commented Anderson.

"Of course," Lester said, grinning. "Odette's as friendly as I am. And Holly made her feel comfortable."

"That's who she is, once you get to know her."

"Yeah, I can see that," Lester said. "We should hang out more often with our ladies."

"I'd like that," Anderson said.

Lester lifted his drink. "Looks like you two have gotten over that bump."

"Pretty much," Anderson agreed.

"Does that mean you're ready to put a ring on her finger?" Lester met his eyes.

Anderson sat back. "It means I'm getting closer…"

"What's the delay? It sure looks to me like Holly's ready and willing to become Mrs. Anderson Gunn."

"But I'm not so sure that she's mentally ready," Anderson said thoughtfully. "I want it to be totally right in her mind and for her to be free of any thoughts of what happened between me and Madison."

Lester frowned. "I don't see how she can't think about that," he said. "Wouldn't you if the situation were reversed?"

"Yeah, but—"

"No buts. It's a normal thing. Doesn't mean it has to be a deal breaker, though. Holly knows how you feel about her. So don't let fear hold you back. Your situation with Madison was different. You're with someone now you're meant to be with. Go ahead and make an honest woman out of her, and then she and Odette can really become good friends."

Anderson grinned. "Not to mention you'd get to play best man."

Lester chuckled. "Yeah, that too."

"We'll see what we can do about that," Anderson said. He still wanted to wait for the perfect time to ask Holly to be his bride. He didn't want her to think of him as anything but one hundred percent committed to them. But would she also be totally committed?

Anderson looked up and saw Holly and Odette coming. He and Lester stood to greet them.

"Miss us?" Holly asked playfully as Anderson gave her a kiss and Lester did the same to Odette.

"Just a little," Anderson said lightly, pulling Holly's chair out for her.

Holly whispered in his ear, "We can do something about that at your place."

He felt his libido kick in. "Music to my ears."

Holly couldn't wait to seduce him tonight and explore every inch of his body. But it was his mind that captured her imagination even more. Anderson seemed to embody virtually all of the qualities she wanted in a strong man, both in bed and out. The only thing missing was whether they would ever become man and wife like Lester and Odette. Had their relationship rubbed off on him the right way? Or did he see the institution of marriage as something that cramped his style?

Holly had her doubts about marrying Anderson. She definitely loved him enough to be his wife. But she wanted to feel in her heart that they were totally on the same wavelength. She wasn't interested in going the divorce route like Blythe. Or never even getting that far, like what had happened to Madison.

Holly felt the gentle squeeze of Anderson's firm hand on her knee. She offered him a warm smile to let him know that she was his before turning her attention to the stage as the singer crooned another jazz standard.

Holly lay on top of Anderson's hard body, kissing him deeply while he impaled her with his erection, exciting every inch of her body. She loved the feel of him inside her; squeezing his manhood and giving Anderson that much more pleasure. His breaths quickened as she lifted up, then lowered herself all the way, again and again, sending waves of electricity throughout her body in the process. She ached from the pleasure and passion, feverishly kissing and sucking his lips while breathing in his masculine scent and woodsy cologne.

Her climax came in guttural waves, and Holly found herself unable to hold back as her body gyrated and quavered astride Anderson, who was drenched in sweat. She pushed her breasts into his face, so that he could lick her nipples as the waves of orgasm continued, taking her to a new level of sexual satisfaction. Finally, she fell atop Anderson, deliriously spent. He was still wedged tightly inside her, having reached his own powerful climax simultaneously.

When the mutual joy was over, Holly rolled off him and placed her head on his chest with one leg draped across his as she breathed in the gratifying scent of their sex. Neither of them uttered a word, content in their union for this night. Holly wanted only to sleep now, as she looked forward to tomorrow and yet more passion that promised to come their way.

The next day, Anderson went with Holly to help with the toy drive. He admired how poised she was and how happy she was to engage people who showed up with toys, even allowing photographs to be taken with her or signing autographs—all for a great cause.

"You really know how to work a gathering," he told her.

"Practice makes perfect," she said, smiling as a car drove up and toys were handed to her. "This is my third year participating, and I love it. It fits right in with my involvement with child literacy."

Anderson took the toys from her and placed them

in a large box. "I couldn't agree more—you are a natural at this."

"So are you," Holly said sincerely. "People feel just as comfortable having you lend your time to do this."

"I wouldn't have it any other way," he said.

"Neither would I," Holly said and kissed him softly on the lips to show her appreciation. Still vivid in her mind was their zealous lovemaking last night, when neither of them had seemed able to get enough of the other. She simply couldn't help herself when it came to wanting him day and night. The fact that it was clear he wanted her every bit as much made it all the more powerful to Holly.

Whether this became a permanent arrangement still remained to be seen. But she would not allow things that were beyond her control to detract from what their love was now.

On Wednesday afternoon, Anderson worked the phones, conferring with his clients. He had become quite comfortable advising other attorneys on how to run their businesses smoothly and efficiently while maximizing their profits. He didn't miss one bit the high stress and long hours of corporate law. Indeed, it was his hope that in a few years he could cut back even more and live off some smart investments, which would give him more time to enjoy his private life. He hoped Holly would always be an important part of his life.

So far, he saw no indication that she didn't want the same things he did. He understood that Holly's work was important to her, and he would never seek to undermine that. If they were to get married and children were to come along, he would happily be a stay-at-home husband and father, doting over his kids the way his mother had doted over him. Whatever way Holly wanted to go, Anderson was ready to jump right in.

I love her like no other and I'll do whatever it takes to prove that to her, he thought. *Making Holly my wife would be a giant and positive step for both of us.*

Anderson would proudly walk down the aisle this time around and he hoped to get that opportunity with Holly. He was snapped from his reverie when his assistant buzzed him. John Lacey, the private investigator, had arrived for their scheduled appointment.

"Send him in," Anderson told her and got to his feet, buttoning his blazer. He was a tad nervous to see John, who apparently had made a breakthrough in his search for Anderson's father.

"Good to see you again," John said, briefcase in hand.

Anderson shook his hand. "You too."

"As I told you over the phone, I have information that I wanted to present to you in person."

"All right." Anderson could not read the man's face enough to get a clue as to what direction this was headed. "Have a seat."

They both sat at the table, and Anderson felt his pulse racing. Was his father alive or dead? If he was alive, was he approachable?

John sighed and looked directly at Anderson. "I've

located your father, Chester Gunn," he said calmly.
"He's alive and well, living just outside of Dallas."

"Really?" Anderson took a moment to let that settle in.

"Yes. He was hard to track down, since he has apparently lived in several states over the years before
settling in the Dallas area."

"Well, is he married? Does he have a family? What
does he do for a living? Or is he retired?" Anderson had
so many questions; he could barely contain his curiosity. Or his indignation that the man had been so close
but had chosen to stay out of his life for all these years.

"Yes, he's married," John said. "As far as I know, he
has no kids…other than you. He's a retired salesman."

Anderson sucked in a deep breath as his piqued interest turned into skepticism. "How do you know this
is the right person? I mean, do I need to take a DNA
test or something?"

"That's something you may want to do at some point,
if it'll give you peace of mind, but I'm fairly certain
we have the right person." He opened up his briefcase
and removed papers. "This Chester Gunn was living
in Houston during the time you were born and is in the
right age range. Twenty years ago he was arrested for
a DUI. Take a look at his mug shot—"

Anderson took the picture from him, studying it.

"When I first saw it," John said, "all I could see was
your face."

Anderson had to agree—it was the spitting image of
him. It had to be his father. So what now? Did he follow through and go to see him?

He had little doubt that Holly would want him to finish what he started. And why shouldn't he? He had to do it, if only for his mother's memory and the man she must have loved at some point.

John seemed to read his mind. "Now that you have information on what in all likelihood is your old man, I suggest you pay him a visit. Maybe he'll be able to fill in some of the blanks in your life or otherwise give you some closure."

"Yeah, I'm sure that's what I'll do," Anderson said.

John took a folder out of the briefcase and put it on the table. "All the information you need is in here."

Anderson nodded. "How much do I owe you?"

"You've covered that." John stood and grabbed the briefcase. "Hope it all works out for you."

"Thanks." Anderson stood. "I appreciate that you found him, for better or worse."

"That's my job. If you ever need my services again, don't hesitate to get in touch."

"I won't." Anderson shook his hand and showed him to the door. Then he asked his assistant to make arrangements for him and Holly to fly to Dallas. He hoped Holly would want to come with him, since he needed her presence to strengthen him as he embarked on this journey to meet his father for the first time.

Chapter 18

Holly went jogging after spending a couple of hours at the station. She took measured breaths, pacing herself as she began the final sprint toward her house. Anderson had promised to start running with her, and she was scheduled to accompany him to the gym next week. Either way, it seemed as though there were plenty of ways for them to get good workouts together, apart from having sex, though she could think of no way more pleasurable.

When she neared the house, Holly spotted the familiar silver Mercedes in the driveway. A smile spread across her face. She had spoken to Anderson a couple of hours ago, and he had never indicated he was dropping by. Not that he needed an excuse, as she loved seeing him whenever she could.

"Hey," she said at the driver's-side window.

"Hey." Anderson smiled and held her shoulder while kissing her lips.

Holly enjoyed the kiss, but pulled back. "Nice, but I'm all sweaty."

"I'm getting used to it and it turns me on," he admitted.

"If you say so." She felt the same way about him when he was hot and sweaty after a long session of lovemaking.

Anderson checked his desire to take her the moment they stepped inside.

"What are you doing here?" Holly asked, sensing something was up.

Anderson waited till they were inside the house before telling her, "I found my father…"

Holly had been hoping for the best but fearing the worst, knowing how challenging it would be to find someone after more than thirty years. She poured him a glass of wine and listened as he talked about the private investigator and where his probing had led.

"I'm so happy for you," she said.

Anderson smiled. "Thanks for giving me a kick in the butt to track him down."

"That's what girlfriends are for."

"In that case, I'm damned lucky I have you as my girlfriend."

"Ditto." She took his glass and tasted the wine. "So are you going to see him?"

"Tomorrow." Anderson gazed at her. "And I'd like you to come with me to Dallas."

"Really?"

"Yes. I have no idea how it might turn out and I could use a strong support system." He sipped the wine. "I know it's short notice and I'll understand if—"

"I'd love to go with you. I'm honored that you want me there when you see your father for the first time," she told him.

Anderson grinned. "Thank you."

"Whatever happens, we'll deal with it together."

"I like that," he said. In more ways than one, he believed that they had what it took to go the distance in life. He saw that with more and more clarity every time he was with her.

"Good." Holly kissed him lightly. "I'm going to hop into the shower. We can talk more afterward."

Anderson grabbed her hand before she could get away. "Care for some company?"

"Hmm…" She could see where this was leading and could think of no reason why they shouldn't go there. "What do you think?"

He flashed a sexy smile, happy to take his mind off the uncertain meeting tomorrow for more immediate gratification.

"I think that's a yes," he told Holly, looking forward to soaping her body, and much more.

As the plane began its descent into the Dallas/Fort Worth International Airport, Holly couldn't help but think how far they had come since she and Anderson had first laid eyes on one another in Portland. She could never have imagined that the exchange would lead to them becoming an item and spending many of their nights and days together. Now they were taking on a new chapter in going to meet his father. Holly had no illusions that it would be the warm, cuddly bond from the start that she had with her father. She was hopeful, though, that Anderson would give him a chance and vice versa.

Anderson was thinking about life, love, marriage and family. He believed these were equally important and wanted to do right by Holly. He wished his mother was still around to see that he had managed well over the years and had found someone who seemed to be every bit as much in his corner as she had been.

"My mother would have adored you," he told Holly.

"I could say the same about my mother and you," she said, holding his hand.

He met her eyes. "Yeah?"

"She was a good judge of character, and she also believed that I would meet a man one day who would sweep me off my feet."

A broad grin crossed Anderson's face. "I think I would've loved your mother for being so insightful."

"I have a feeling that our mothers are looking down on us, satisfied that we found each other," Holly said. She suspected that their mothers would want to see them married and settled down, something that she also wanted. But not until Anderson was fully prepared to take that important step in their relationship.

"I'm sure you're right," Anderson said. He knew her father was in his corner, too. But what about his father? Would he come away from this meeting with a new family member who would want to remain in their lives?

They rented a car and drove through the culturally diverse city, passing by the Thanksgiving Square, Dealey Plaza and Dallas Arboretum—all of which Holly had visited in the past—till they arrived at a two-story red-brick home.

"This is it," Anderson said, pulling alongside the curb. Though he had a phone number, he opted not to use it, figuring this was something that needed to be done face-to-face.

"Looks like someone's home," Holly said, noting there were two cars in the driveway.

"Guess there's no turning back now," Anderson said.

"Do you know what you're going to say to him?"

"Whatever comes to mind in that moment," he said uneasily. "Let's go meet my dad."

They walked up to the house and Anderson hesitated as the jitters hit him. Had he really come to Dallas to visit the man who had fathered him but had never cared enough to even acknowledge his existence?

He sucked in a deep breath, steeling himself to go for it.

He rang the doorbell.

The door opened and Anderson recognized the man standing there as the same one he had seen in the mug shot.

Chester Gunn was in his sixties, bald and of medium build but close to Anderson's height. He could well imagine that he was looking at an older future version of himself.

"Are you Chester Gunn?" Anderson asked.

"Yes, I'm Chester Gunn." He eyed Anderson. "How can I help you?"

Anderson felt his heart skip a beat in that moment, where everything could change forever.

"Do you remember Diane Lockhart?" Anderson asked him.

Chester paused. "Yes, we dated a long time ago. Why?"

"She was my mother." Anderson regarded him squarely. "My name is Anderson Gunn. I believe you're my father—"

Chester studied him for a long moment, his face crinkled with shock. "You're telling me you're my son?"

"I have good reason to think I am," Anderson said.

Chester ran a hand across his mouth and then turned to Holly. "Who are you?"

"Holly Kendall," she said. "I'm Anderson's girlfriend."

Chester faced him again. "Come in."

Anderson looked at Holly, who gave him a supportive smile, before taking the man up on his offer.

They stood in the living room, which was small, with leather furnishings and a carpeted floor.

"Sit down," Chester told them.

Anderson and Holly sat on the sofa and watched as Chester sat in a chair across from them.

"Where's your mother?" Chester asked.

Anderson frowned. "She's been dead for many years."

"I'm sorry to hear that," Chester said. "You've got my eyes and nose."

And your genes, Anderson thought. He was still unsure how he felt at this point but wondered what his old man had to say for himself about abandoning him and his mother.

"Guess I took after you more than my mother," he said.

"How did you find me?" Chester asked.

"I hired a good private detective."

"Why, after all these years?" he asked.

Anderson turned toward Holly and thought about her close-knit relationship with her father before facing him again. "It seemed like a good idea to try to find out if you were still alive."

"I see." Chester sat back. "I never thought I'd lay eyes on you again."

"Why didn't you ever look for me?" Anderson asked curtly. "Why did you leave my mother pregnant and alone?"

Holly squeezed his hand, knowing how hard this was for Anderson. She only hoped the answers were something he could live with.

"Your mother and I had a falling out back then," Chester said, gripping the armrest. "Neither of us was exclusive in the relationship. When I learned she was pregnant, I offered to marry her, believing the child to be mine. But she told me it was another man's kid."

"Why would she do that?" Anderson asked skeptically.

"It was her way of getting back at me for seeing other women. Never mind the fact that she saw just as many other men."

"That doesn't make any sense," Anderson said.

"It was the type of give-and-take relationship we had," Chester said, sighing. "When your mother was pissed about something, she could be pretty damned vindictive. After you were born, I again tried to stake my claim to you, but by then Diane was in a relationship with the man she said was your father. I left town shortly after that, never knowing what became of them or you."

Anderson tried to come to grips with what he'd just heard. He remembered that there had been a string of men in and out of his mother's life—mostly out. But she had always insisted that the only one she'd ever truly loved was his father. Why hadn't she been straight with him?

How could she hide the fact that his father had been misled as well? Why not make peace with him and admit he had a child before it was too late?

Anderson wasn't sure what to think, but was inclined to believe that his mother had, for whatever reason, chosen to deny him his father—perhaps as some ill-advised way of punishing his father.

"Guess I owe you an apology," Anderson said. He looked carefully at Chester and thought of all the years they had lost.

"You don't owe me anything," Chester responded. "None of this was your fault. I probably should have tried harder to get the truth out of your mother, but at the time I was hurting and just wanted to get on with my life."

"So what now?" Anderson asked.

Holly trained her eyes on Chester, waiting to see how he would react to the opening offered by Anderson. She had not expected this turn of events. Apparently Anderson's mother had misled him and his father wasn't a deadbeat after all. He was only an aging man who had just found out he had a son.

"I'd like us to get to know one another," Chester said. "How do you feel about it?"

"I'd like that," Anderson said. He was fighting back tears.

Chester smiled. "Then we'll make sure it happens." He looked at Holly. "It would be nice to get to know your girlfriend, too."

"I'd like that," Holly said, blushing. She could even imagine their fathers becoming friends.

Just then the front door opened and an attractive woman in her mid-fifties entered. She looked at Chester. "I didn't know we had company."

Chester stood up. "This is my wife, Patrice," he said. "That's Anderson and his girlfriend, Holly." He paused. "Anderson is my son…."

"Never quite saw that coming," Anderson said on the plane back to Houston. They had spent the afternoon with his father and stepmother, catching up on each other's lives.

"Life can be full of surprises," Holly said.

"I'll never be able to figure my mother out. What was she thinking?"

"For some things there are no easy answers," Holly suggested. "Maybe she had what she thought were valid reasons for not telling you the truth about your father."

"Or maybe it was all done out of spite, even if at my expense," Anderson said.

"Whatever was going on in her head, I'm sure she loved you." Holly wanted to believe that much at least.

"Yeah," Anderson conceded. If nothing else, aside from gaining a new family, this allowed him to take stock of his own life and his future with the woman he loved.

Anderson now knew what he needed to do to have the type of romance and family that his parents had been denied. The only question was whether or not Holly was ready to hear what he had to say.

Chapter 19

When they arrived at her house, Holly had expected Anderson to walk her to the door and kiss her goodbye. He had told her that he needed to get some work done in preparation for a meeting in the morning.

But he asked to come in and she was more than happy to have him, figuring they might have a nightcap and even make love, if he had the time.

Anderson regarded Holly, still wowed by her beauty and grace. He put his hands on her waist and stared into those wonderful eyes. "Thank you for accompanying me to see my father. It meant a lot."

"It did to me, too," she promised. "I'm glad that it had a good ending and a new beginning at the same time."

"So am I." He paused. "Marry me."

"What...?" Holly fluttered her lashes.

"I want us to get married," he said. "I love you, Holly, and I want you to be my wife. I hope you'll make me the happiest man in the world by saying yes."

Holly sucked in a deep breath, taking in the words she had waited to hear from him for some time. And yet, while she very much wanted to be his wife, she hesitated to say yes.

"You know I love you, Anderson, and asking me to marry you is a magical thing..."

He sensed a "but" coming, and his heart sank. "Magical enough to become my bride?"

She met his steady gaze and knew she had to ask. "Why now?" Was it a reaction to his parents' failure to marry and do right by him? Or to prove to himself that he could actually follow through on a marriage proposal?

Anderson's brows knitted. "Why now? Because it felt like the right time to put it on the table."

"That sounds more like a business proposition than a declaration of love and devotion."

"I'm not making a business proposition to you," he tried to assure her. "You have my love and devotion."

"Like Madison did?"

"Can't we just keep her out of this?" Anderson had hoped his ex would be a thing of the past at this stage of their relationship.

Holly sighed. As much as she wanted to believe that what happened to Madison wasn't relevant to his proposal, she felt it was very much so. That old saying "what goes around, comes around" registered in her mind. Had he truly gotten the jitters of marriage out of his system? Or would it rear its ugly head once more, no matter his good intentions?

"It's hard not to think about what Madison went through," Holly said, feeling him loosen his hands from her waist. "How can I be sure you'll follow through this time?"

Anderson's nostrils flared.

"Look, I know you think I'm proposing halfheartedly," he said evenly. "But I'm not. I wasn't ready to marry Madison and realized that before it was too late. With you, it's definitely the real deal."

Holly wanted so badly to believe him. Becoming Mrs. Anderson Gunn was what she wanted, and it would be the first step toward starting a family. But if he were to break off the engagement, it would break her heart into a million pieces.

"Does this have anything to do with finding your father?" she wondered. "Maybe you just want to do what he should have done?"

Anderson took an involuntary step back. "Do you really believe that?"

"You tell me," she said, folding her arms. "I just want to make sure you're proposing for the right reasons."

"The reasons are right to me," he said with an edge to his voice. "And it's not about my father or my mother. They had their chance to be together and chose not to for whatever reason. I have to respect that, even if it left me in a broken home and eventually with no home at all." He ran his fingers along her chin. "I love you and I want to make it official. Can't that be reason enough?"

"Yes, it should be." Holly closed her eyes as she felt the warmth of his hand on her face, then opened them. *Why am I stalling over something I want?* she thought. *Am I the one who's suddenly getting cold feet?*

"Then what is it?" Anderson demanded. "Are you happier if we just keep a nice sexual relationship going minus the marriage certificate? Would marriage somehow put a crimp in your image as a beautiful, successful and single newscaster?"

Holly's eyes narrowed. "I never said all I wanted from you was a sexual relationship without marriage," she snapped. "And being married would not put a crimp, as you put it, into my professional life. If I'm not rushing to accept your marriage proposal, it's strictly because I want us both to think about it before I give you my answer. That way, if you have any second thoughts, you can tell me beforehand and save us both hurt down the line. I know this isn't what you wanted to hear, but it's how I feel. I'm sorry."

"So am I," Anderson said, trying to keep a cool head. He should have seen this coming. His failed engagement with Madison was going to continue to dog him. Or was that more of a convenient tool Holly was using as an excuse not to marry him? Maybe he was overthinking this. It could be that she legitimately needed more time to weigh this. But she clearly was not ready to accept his offer of marriage. Maybe she never would be.

He lowered his eyes to hers. "Take all the time you need," he said evenly.

"Thank you." Holly hoped he meant it. She didn't want to lose him. But if they couldn't survive a delay in her answer, how would they ever hope to get through the ceremony and maintain a long and happy marriage?

"I'd better go," Anderson said.

"Okay," she agreed softly.

He kissed her on the cheek. "See you later."

Holly watched him walk away, almost feeling as though she had lost her best friend. She wanted things to work out without the shadow of past mistakes hanging over them. Was that possible?

Two days later, Holly had drinks with Blythe at the Carnation Lounge on Louisiana Street.

"I think it was a smart move to think it over before saying yes or no," Blythe said, sipping a cocktail. "I mean, it's not like he hasn't gone down that road before."

"I know," Holly said. "But I think he truly loves me."

"Isn't that what your friend thought, too, once upon a time?" Blythe reminded her. "All I'm saying is that it's better to err on the side of caution than to jump in headfirst and suffer the consequences."

Holly agreed, which was partially why she had held off giving Anderson an answer. It was a chance she had to take. Then there was also the small part of her that needed to be absolutely positive that she was ready to become a wife, even to someone she dearly loved.

"I shou... Nowaday... Blythe said, "having been there my-self. no strings attache... ppy just dating a nice guy with

"But I want the str... said. "As long as I don't los... lls and whistles," Holly the process." ...part of who I am in

"You're too smart to let that happen, ...the told her. "Much smarter than I was when I got married. The real question is if you agree to marry him, will Anderson bother to show up at the wedding?"

Holly stared into space thoughtfully while sipping her drink. In her heart, she was certain that Anderson would not allow history to repeat itself. But that didn't mean her heart wouldn't be racing a mile a minute until it became official.

"What's meant to be will be," she finally said. "Anderson and I have pretty much been on the same page on most fronts. Even though getting married is a big step, if it's something we both really want to happen, nothing should stand in the way."

"That's true in fantasyland or a romance novel," Blythe said. "Unfortunately, the best-laid plans do not always materialize in the real world."

Holly's brows furrowed. "You think what we have is a fantasy?"

"No, not at all," she stressed. "You obviously care for one another deeply. I just want you to keep a clear head when you make your decision, and that you be-lieve in your heart that it's the right one."

Holly considered Blythe's words. She knew that a

lot of this also rested on Ander... ...ulders. He had
to remain comfortable with... ...sire to marry her,
especially now that she b... ...poned her decision on
whether to accept his... ...sal.

She would ha... ...hink a lot about it and hope he
would be gra... ...s if the marriage was never to happen
between ...m.

"Can you blame her for holding back just a little?"
Lester said, as they sat on the balcony at Anderson's
apartment.

Anderson put a beer bottle to his mouth and took a
drink. "Probably not," he conceded. "But she has absolutely nothing to fear. I love her to death and have no
intention of backing out of the marriage."

"I'm sure you believe that and, for the record, I believe it, too," Lester said. "But once you've established
a track record to the contrary, it stays with you, like it
or not. The fact that Madison and Holly happen to be
friends who can compare notes probably doesn't help
matters any either."

"Madison's not around anymore," Anderson said.
He'd heard that she had moved to Portland, and he was
glad that they could put some distance between them,
as well as between her and Holly.

"That helps," Lester said. "But it really comes down
to how much you've impressed upon Holly that your
love and desire to marry her go hand in hand, and that
she can count on it as sure as the sun rising."

Anderson chuckled uneasily. "I'm not sure the impression I've left has been all that strong."

"I'd say just the opposite. From what I've seen, you and Holly are definitely in love. The fact that she didn't accept your proposal right away is actually a good thing."

"For whom?" Anderson asked.

"For you," Lester told him. He grabbed some potato chips from a bag. "Most women like to play hardball just so you don't take anything for granted. That includes a marriage proposal. Besides, it'll give you the chance to do it right."

Anderson looked at him. "Meaning…?"

"Meaning a nice big engagement ring, down on one knee, the whole works. All the old-fashioned stuff that we think we can bypass these days."

"I get your point," Anderson said.

"Good. So do what you need to do and wait for her to respond," Lester said. "I have a feeling you won't be disappointed."

Anderson wanted nothing more than to make Holly happy in every way. Even if that meant lying low and giving her the space she needed until she was ready to spend the rest of her life as Mrs. Anderson Gunn.

On Friday morning Holly went for a bike ride, trying to stick to her exercise routine even if her mind was elsewhere. More specifically, it was stuck on her man. At least, she assumed she was still the love of Anderson's life, since he was the love of hers. They had only texted for the past three days and she was missing the warmth of his touch like crazy, along with the deep and soothing sound of his voice.

So call him, she told herself. No reason to wait for him to call her—she was every bit as invested in the relationship as he was.

By the time she got home, showered and dressed, Holly had come to the conclusion that she needed Anderson in each and every way, including as her husband, best friend and lifetime partner. His past was not a prelude to their future. Asking for her hand in marriage was something she was sure he had given much thought. Meeting him halfway would show her trust in him and her commitment to sharing a wonderful life together.

She drove to Anderson's loft, taking a chance that he would be there. *I can't wait any longer to tell him what he wants to hear,* she thought excitedly.

Anderson was doing a little work online when the bell rang. He looked at his security monitor and saw Holly's lovely face. He buzzed her in.

Keep your cool and don't have any expectations, he thought.

He opened the door and smiled. "Hey."

"Hi." Holly grinned. He never seemed to have a bad day in the looks department, which made her all the more attracted to him.

"Can I get you something to drink?" Anderson asked. "Or eat?"

"Do you still want to marry me?" Holly blurted out.

"Absolutely." Anderson held her gaze. "I love you and want to make it official."

She beamed. "Then yes, I will marry you."

"You will? Hold that thought—" He held up a hand, barely able to contain his exhilaration.

Anderson went to the countertop in the kitchen where he'd left the little box with a big ring inside. He grabbed it and returned to Holly, determined to do this right.

Opening the box, he said, "This is the ring you deserved all along..."

He removed a 2.5-carat marquise diamond bordered by baguette diamonds before falling to one knee and taking her hand. He slipped the ring on her finger. "Will you marry me, Holly Kendall?"

She locked eyes with him.

"Why, yes, Anderson Gunn, I will marry you." She chuckled, then looked in awe at the huge center stone and the sparkling side stones.

He got to his feet. "Those words are the sweetest music to my ears," he murmured.

"And mine." Anderson held her cheeks and planted a solid kiss on her lips. Holly, not to be outdone, extended the kiss by wrapping her arms around his neck to savor the wonderful moment.

Chapter 20

Anderson sat in the club seats at Reliant Stadium beside Robert and Chester, taking in a Houston Texans game. As hoped, the home team was leading at the start of the second half and the crowd was cheering raucously.

"Let's just see if we can hold them off a little while longer," Robert said.

"I'll drink to that," Chester said, lifting his beer as the two men toasted to victory.

Anderson grinned. He felt good about the bonding experience that suddenly had him with not one, but two fathers to form a relationship with. He was ready and willing to make a go of it for himself and Holly. She was big on family and so was he, now that he had one.

He looked up and saw Holly returning from the ladies' room. Standing, Anderson greeted her with a kiss.

"I didn't miss anything, did I?" she asked.

"Not really," he said. "But I sure as hell missed you."

Her lashes fluttered and she kissed him again. "Remind me again of just how lucky I am."

Anderson beamed. "That makes us equally lucky to have found one another."

They sat and conversed with their fathers, before the men once again became distracted with the game.

Holly was certainly enjoying this family outing and wished Stuart and the girls were there. She was confident that they would visit soon and that she and Anderson would visit them in Portland. After all, it was a visit to Portland that had led to their whirlwind romance, and now she couldn't be happier.

Actually, she could, once they were officially Mr. and Mrs. Anderson Gunn. They were still working to set a wedding date. In Holly's mind, the sooner she could become Anderson's wife, the better. In spite of some lingering thoughts about his failed engagement to Madison, she was confident that their journey into matrimony would be smooth sailing.

"Now what's going on in that pretty head of yours?" Anderson asked Holly, noticing that she was clearly distracted.

She smiled at him. "Oh, I'm just trying to decide if we should put up the Christmas decorations at your place or mine this year, since we're spending practically all of our time together at one place or the other."

"Why not both?" he suggested. "In the spirit of the season, decorating both of our places can be twice as nice."

"Agreed," she said. Now the question was, what did she get a man for Christmas who had everything?

Maybe I'll wrap myself up with a bow as his gift, she thought with amusement, certain he would love to unwrap her and do as he pleased with his gift.

On Christmas day, Anderson planted a big kiss on Holly's mouth as they stood beneath the mistletoe in her living room, the beautifully decorated tree in the backdrop. He had been looking forward to this moment for days and made the most of it, holding her snugly in his arms as their open mouths devoured one another desirously.

Holly was blown away from the potent kiss that left her breathless. She clung to her fiancé, their bodies molded together, as the heat of the kiss raised her temperature.

After kissing for several minutes, Anderson reluctantly pulled away. "Merry Christmas, darling," he murmured, gazing into her eyes.

"Merry Christmas back at you, baby," she said, her lips still tingling.

"What do you think of a Valentine's Day wedding?" he asked.

Holly met his gaze. "I think it sounds incredibly romantic."

"My thoughts precisely," Anderson said. "What could be more appropriate and memorable than tying the knot on a day that celebrates love and devotion between sweethearts?"

Holly's face lit up; she was enamored with the idea. "So let's get married on Valentine's Day!" she declared.

Anderson couldn't wait to exchange vows with Holly, knowing that she was the woman he truly wanted to wed and spend the rest of his life with.

They kissed again for an even longer stretch, before opening their Christmas gifts and making plans for the upcoming New Year's Day celebration.

On Valentine's Day, Holly was a bundle of nerves. The wedding was only an hour away. Gone were any doubts she had once had that Anderson wouldn't show up. She knew he loved her and wanted to become her husband as much as she wanted to be his wife. But she was wound up for all the normal reasons on a wedding day: would the minister show up on time, would she re-member her vows, would she trip while walking down the aisle, would the reception go off as planned without a hitch, and more…

Just calm down, she told herself, taking a deep breath as she slipped into her dress. *People go through this all the time and everything seems to work out.* She knew she had to let the process play itself out and it would be over before she knew it, with her becoming the wife of the man she loved dearly.

"You look amazing!" Blythe said as she entered the dressing room at the church.

Holly got to see for herself as she stood before a full-length mirror. She wore an ivory charmeuse gown with cap sleeves and a lace bodice. Her hair was up and fitted with a metal rhinestone headband that had a side floral motif. The two-tiered veil had beaded flowers and lace. A pearl-and-diamond necklace and teardrop earrings added sparkle. Ivory peep-toe high heels completed her outfit.

"I do look pretty damned good, don't I?" she couldn't help but say. She felt like Cinderella waiting for her Prince Charming to make her life complete.

Blythe chuckled. "Just imagine what Anderson will think when he sees you. The man will be floored."

"I hope so." Holly wanted to wow him the way she expected Anderson would wow her. She suspected there would be even more excitement when they got to remove each other's clothing tonight after the wedding and reception.

"Well, let's not keep him waiting," Blythe said, handling her role as the matron of honor flawlessly.

"Let's not," Holly seconded, eager to become his bride and start a new life together.

Anderson felt warm as he stood in front of the church in his designer cream-colored tuxedo. He had probably never been more nervous in his life, and wouldn't have wanted it any other way. There were no second thoughts in his mind about marrying Holly. Quite the contrary, he wanted her to be his wife more than ever, and he knew in his heart and soul that she was the woman he was meant to be with as a devoted husband and future family man. The sooner they made it official, the sooner they could begin the next chapter in their lives as newlyweds.

"Well, this is it," his best man, Lester, said, patting him on the shoulder. "Your big day!"

"I'm ready for it," Anderson assured him. "I couldn't be happier."

Lester grinned. "I think you will be when you see your bride-to-be coming our way…"

Anderson turned his head and saw Holly being led down the aisle by Robert. She had never looked more beautiful. She flashed him a thousand-watt smile, and he went weak in the knees. He wasn't sure what he'd done to deserve her in his life, but would do it again and again if that was what it took to keep Holly as his one and only.

Holly had her arm beneath her father's as they walked toward Anderson. She tried to keep her pulse from racing as she watched her two young nieces, who were the flower girls. Her brother, Stuart, was all smiles and gave her a reassuring nod.

It was her moment, and Holly basked in it, elated to share her wedding day with so many people.

She stood next to her fiancé, who gave her a toothy grin.

"I love you," he said quietly, his eyes lowered to meet hers.

"I love you, too," she said, trying hard not to cry and ruin her makeup. But the emotion of seeing him now— the picture of svelte perfection in his tux, his confident posture and incredible good looks—was almost too much for her to hold back her tears of happiness. To think that they were moments away from having it all made the occasion all the more joyous.

The minister, a female in her forties, offered them a warm smile. "Are you ready to make this union of your love an official bond?"

"Yes," Holly and Anderson responded in unison.

"Wonderful. Then let's get started…"

Anderson did not flinch when saying what was in his heart to Holly. "I promise to always love you more than life itself and be the man you fell in love with every day. Wherever life takes us, it will be hand in hand."

Holly embraced the tender words, knowing they came from the heart. She trembled slightly when it came time to say her wedding vows, which she had written herself.

"I cannot adequately express how much I love you and want to be your wife and companion," she told Anderson. "You've given me something I've never had before—a person whom I can love and devote the rest of my life to in as many ways as possible. I'm very ready to become your wife."

The minister's eyes crinkled. "In that case, let us exchange wedding rings."

Lester handed Anderson a three-carat diamond cluster ring set in fourteen-karat gold. Anderson placed it on Holly's finger while peering lovingly into her eyes.

Holly could no longer hold back the tears as she slid a two-tone gold wedding band onto Anderson's finger.

He smiled thankfully and they held hands as the minister now pronounced them man and wife. "You may kiss your new bride," she told Anderson.

He did not have to be told twice. He angled his head just right and pressed his mouth to Holly's. She was smiling and crying at once as she kissed him back.

Holly was so caught up in the toe-tingling kiss that she shut out their surroundings and those witnessing the occasion. It wasn't until the minister got their attention that Holly pried her lips from Anderson's.

"I think you two made your point," the minister joked. "May I welcome to everyone Mr. and Mrs. Anderson Gunn."

Anderson and Holly made their way down the aisle, hand in hand, as family and friends cheered them on.

Outside, the newlyweds got into Anderson's Mercedes, hardly able to take their eyes off one another. Holly could scarcely believe that she was now married to the love of her life.

Holly and Anderson flew to the Cayman Islands for their honeymoon, where they soaked up the sun and enjoyed tourist attractions and danced till dark. But much of their time was spent in bed enjoying each other's company and the pleasures of steamy lovemaking as newlyweds.

Having lost herself in their passion, Holly took a deep breath before falling on Anderson, totally spent from their latest round of sex. She kissed him deeply, still reeling from the orgasm he had just given her. She was beginning to believe that sex was even better when you were husband and wife.

Anderson echoed such thoughts. "Maybe we should get ourselves a summer place here so we can always come back for a repeat performance," he said, nibbling at her ear. "Or better yet, maybe we should simply stay in this room and never leave!"

Holly laughed and kissed him again. "That last idea may be the best one you've had yet," she said.

"I thought you might see things my way, Mrs. Gunn." He turned her over and kissed her passionately. "Let's work on that."

Her body tingled with each tantalizing kiss and caress. "Yes, let's…"

* * * * *

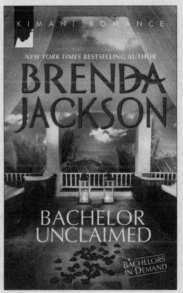

REQUEST YOUR FREE BOOKS!

2 FREE NOVELS
PLUS 2 FREE GIFTS!

KIMANI ROMANCE™

Love's ultimate destination!

YES! Please send me 2 FREE Kimani™ Romance novels and my 2 FREE gifts (gifts are worth about $10). After receiving them, if I don't wish to receive any more books, I can return the shipping statement marked "cancel." If I don't cancel, I will receive 4 brand-new novels every month and be billed just $4.94 per book in the U.S. or $5.49 per book in Canada. That's a savings of at least 21% off the cover price. It's quite a bargain! Shipping and handling is just 50¢ per book in the U.S. and 75¢ per book in Canada.* I understand that accepting the 2 free books and gifts places me under no obligation to buy anything. I can always return a shipment and cancel at any time. Even if I never buy another book, the two free books and gifts are mine to keep forever.

168/368 XDN FVUK

Name   (PLEASE PRINT)

Address   Apt. #

City   State/Prov.   Zip/Postal Code

Signature (if under 18, a parent or guardian must sign)

Mail to the **Harlequin® Reader Service:**

IN U.S.A.: P.O. Box 1867, Buffalo, NY 14240-1867
IN CANADA: P.O. Box 609, Fort Erie, Ontario L2A 5X3

Want to try two free books from another line?
Call 1-800-873-8635 or visit www.ReaderService.com.

* Terms and prices subject to change without notice. Prices do not include applicable taxes. Sales tax applicable in N.Y. Canadian residents will be charged applicable taxes. Offer not valid in Quebec. This offer is limited to one order per household. Not valid for current subscribers to Kimani Romance books. All orders subject to credit approval. Credit or debit balances in a customer's account(s) may be offset by any other outstanding balance owed by or to the customer. Please allow 4 to 6 weeks for delivery. Offer available while quantities last.

Your Privacy—The Harlequin® Reader Service is committed to protecting your privacy. Our Privacy Policy is available online at www.ReaderService.com or upon request from the Harlequin Reader Service.

We make a portion of our mailing list available to reputable third parties that offer products we believe may interest you. If you prefer that we not exchange your name with third parties, or if you wish to clarify or modify your communication preferences, please visit us at www.ReaderService.com/consumerschoice or write to us at Harlequin Reader Service Preference Service, P.O. Box 9062, Buffalo, NY 14269. Include your complete name and address.

KROM13

Three couples celebrate the most romantic day—and night—of the year in....

Valentine's Dream

**SANDRA KITT
CARMEN GREEN
FELICIA MASON**

Three classic tales of love and romance sure to touch your heart...

Fan-Favorite Authors

SANDRA KITT
CARMEN GREEN
FELICIA MASON

For three single women, Valentine's Day proves to be the catalyst for love affairs that none expected. Though these sexy ladies don't believe in love at first sight, will Cupid's arrow head straight for their hearts?